DATE DUE

SEP 1 1 2006		DEC 1 8 2007	
SEP 2 0 2006			
		FEB 0 8 2008	
		MAR 1 9 2008	
OCT 0 3 2006			
		MAR 1 9 2008	
OCT 2 5 2006		JUL 1 2 2008	
NOV 3 0 2006		AUG 0 5 2008	
DEC 2 1 2006		SEP 1 3 2008	
JAN 2 9 2007		OCT 0 7 2008	
MAR 2 5 2007		4-26-11	
JUN 1 9 2007			
AUG 1 1 2007			
NOV 0 4 2007			
NOV 0 5 2007			

Nina Quinn Mysteries
by Heather Webber

Digging up Trouble
Trouble in Spades
A Hoe Lot of Trouble

HEATHER
WEBBER

A NINA QUINN MYSTERY

DIGGING UP TROUBLE

AVON BOOKS
An Imprint of HarperCollins*Publishers*

This is a work of fiction. Names, characters, places, and incidents are products of the author's imagination or are used fictitiously and are not to be construed as real. Any resemblance to actual events, locales, organizations, or persons, living or dead, is entirely coincidental.

AVON BOOKS
An Imprint of HarperCollins*Publishers*
10 East 53rd Street
New York, New York 10022-5299

ISBN-13: 978-0-06-072349-1
ISBN-10: 0-06-072349-1
www.avonmystery.com

First Avon Books paperback printing: April 2006

Printed in the U.S.A.

10 9 8 7 6 5 4 3 2 1

For my family,
who ply me with plenty of story ideas . . .
and hugs.
A great combination.
All my love.

Acknowledgments

Special thanks to my agent, Jacky Sach, for all that you do, and to Sarah Durand, for continuing to believe in Nina . . . and in me.

Great big thanks to Laura Bradford, Shelley Galloway, Hilda Lindner-Knepp, Cathy Liggett, and Julie Stone, for being the best writing buddies a girl could have.

DIGGING UP TROUBLE

One

Thou, Nina Colette Ceceri Quinn, shall not hire any more unreliable ex-cons.

Not an easy commandment, to say the least, since I really couldn't tell who was reliable and who wasn't until they started working for me.

I frowned. Talk about a Catch-22.

The trick was weeding out the good from the bad. As I looked around my office conference room, I realized I'd certainly found a few good ones in Kit Pipe, Deanna Parks, Marty Johnson, and Coby Fowler. And of course Tam Oliver, who sat in her throne chair in the reception area pretending she wasn't eavesdropping.

My business, Taken by Surprise, Garden Designs, had thrived over the last few years because of their hard work. And getting any specialized landscaping business to thrive in this day and age was notable, but here in small-town Freedom, Ohio, it was a miracle. This was middle-class country, the heart of the Midwest, and I charged upper-class prices for my day-in, day-out yard makeovers.

It was the bad experiences with my rap-sheeted workers that made me question my hiring practices. Currently, one worker in particular.

"So, no one's seen him?" I asked, looking down the long rectangular table. It was littered with soda cans, coffee cups, and the sad remains of two dozen Krispy Kremes.

"Not since he left yesterday afternoon." Deanna twirled a pencil like a baton. "Said he had an appointment he couldn't miss. And he was all dolled up too. I smelled him coming through a closed door."

The "he" in question was Jean-Claude Reaux, who tended to wear too much cologne, and who was currently MIA. He'd worked for me three years.

He'd started out as a laborer, but I soon noticed he had an uncanny instinct for finding unique items and fabrics to go with my designs. He still did labor—we all did—but now he had a lot more input on these design meetings.

Like the one we were in now.

Like the one he hadn't shown up for.

"We can't wait much longer," Kit put in. Kit was my right-hand man.

I found myself staring at him. Not because he was six-foot-five, 250 pounds. Or that his eyes had been tattooed with dark liner sometime in the late eighties. It was because I couldn't get used to the sight of him with hair.

Hair, of all things.

This from a man who practically spit-shined the skull tattoo on his bald head. The tattoo now covered with downy soft-looking brown fuzz.

"Stop staring," he said.

"I can't help it."

He growled. "Try."

"I kind of like it," Deanna said.

Lord, was she blushing? I groaned. I didn't need Deanna having a crush on Kit. Interoffice romances were somewhat prohibited (I'd been known to bend the rules), but that wasn't why. It was because I really didn't want to see anything happen to Deanna—Kit's live-in girlfriend, Daisy, was the jealous type.

Or so I'd heard. No one had ever seen her. Not even once.

Which certainly piqued my nosiness.

"Me too," Coby singsonged, and batted his eyelashes.

Kit's eyes narrowed. In a dangerous whisper he said, "See what you did?"

"Me?" I asked. "What did I do?"

"You stared."

"Oh for heaven's sake. Sue me." At Kit's growl, I rushed on. "So, where were we?"

"Staring." Deanna's cheeks were still rosy.

Kit crushed a Mountain Dew can.

I ignored him and riffled through the papers in the file in front of me. "No, before that."

"Jean-Claude," Marty supplied, reaching for another Krispy Kreme.

"Oh yeah."

"This isn't the first time he's been a no-show," Kit reminded.

No, it wasn't. So far this month, Jean-Claude had come in late twice and hadn't bothered to show at all three times. Four if you counted today.

Not a good track record. Especially considering we were only two weeks into July.

Any sane boss would fire him.

Unfortunately, I'd come to recognize in my twenty-nine years that I leaned to the right side of normal.

"No one knows what he's up to?" I asked, looking for some explanation. "Marty?"

"Me?" he mumbled over a mouth full of glazed doughnut.

The phone rang in the front room, and I heard Tam answer it. Maybe it was Jean-Claude? Calling in? With a doozy of an excuse?

Because if he didn't have a doozy of an excuse, I really would have to fire him.

Sooner or later.

Sooner probably if Kit's glare was any indication.

Inwardly I groaned. I hated firing people.

Tam stuck her head in the door. "Nina?"

I looked up, hopeful. "Is that Jean-Claude?"

She shook her head, her tight curls not budging. "No. It's Lindsey Lockhart. She said she's running late and won't be able to make it until ten. Is that okay?"

My hands immediately turned damp. "Yeah. That's fine. We're running behind here anyway."

"Okay." She turned slowly and walked away, her belly leading. Tam was due in five weeks, and I didn't know what I was going to do without her while she was on maternity leave.

I thought back to my newest commandment and wondered if I should hire a temp through a reputable agency. Only that might ruffle Ana's feathers. My cousin Ana Bertoli was a probation officer who sent me her probationers when someone had trouble finding a job or if I needed a new hire.

Ana would live if I hired a temp. I'd live too.

Probably. Hopefully.

"Jean-Claude," Kit reminded me when I looked down at my file.

Deanna twirled her pencil baton. "I can take over his workload for tomorrow's makeover."

"I can pitch in too," Marty chimed in, picking doughnut crumbs from the napkin in front of him with dark fingers.

"Me too," Coby offered.

I looked at Kit. "It's a given," he said.

And it was. I could count on Kit for anything. That's why I had to be careful with this newest commandment. I had hired a lot of great people over the years, criminal records and all.

I still lumped Jean-Claude into that group. For now. Until a month ago he'd been a model employee. Sure, he had his dark side, but as long as I didn't ask, he didn't tell. It hadn't affected his work, and that's all I truly cared about.

I was lying.

I tended to do that, which was why I hadn't made it a commandment yet. I knew I couldn't keep it.

I cared about more than Jean-Claude's work—I cared about him. Add that to my worrier nature and I knew I was in trouble. What was going on with him?

"Why is Mrs. Lockhart coming here? Don't you usually meet clients at their homes, or rather their yards, for the final walk-through?" Deanna asked, tossing her pencil up in the air.

That pencil was seriously getting on my nerves.

"Usually, yes, but she requested the meeting here. I didn't see why not." It was just as well. Being here in comfortable surroundings might make it easier for me to quiz the woman.

She held the answers to some burning questions I had.

"Could be her husband was going to be home."

Kit had a point. Surprise garden makeovers (surprise being the key word) were the objective of Taken by Surprise.

"Let's not dwell on it," I said. "Jean-Claude was in charge of the tree and shrub selection for this project, as well as accessories."

Deanna balanced the pencil on the tip of her index finger. "I think he said something about an old wishing well he'd found."

"I saw it out in the shed," Marty said.

Oooh. A wishing well would be a perfect complement to this project. The older and more rustic-looking, the better.

See, this was why I hated to lose Jean-Claude.

He'd better have a damn good excuse.

After checking my list, I turned to Deanna. "Azaleas, rhododendrons, hydrangeas, right?"

"Right. To go with your blue and white theme, I picked up some bellflowers, belladonna delphiniums, blue balloon flowers, blue chip campanula, and butterfly blue scabiosa, white dragonflower, white bleeding heart, and Deutschland astilbe," she said, actually using the pencil to tick off the list on the pad of paper in front of her.

"Sounds great."

"Stanley checked in this morning. The deck is on schedule," Kit said.

"And you'll be helping him with that, right?"

"That and the seating once the excavating work is done."

"Coby? What're you doing?"

"Fire pit and lighting."

That's right. "Got everything?"

"Yes."

"Kit, have you checked in with Ignacio? Is he all set?"

Ignacio Martinez was a floater. He and his crew of workers drifted between different jobs, working where there was money to be had. Sometimes they did landscaping, other times bricklaying or general construction. I hired Ignacio and his crew for particularly tough yards. They were worth every cent I paid them under the table.

I scanned my notes. "The sod and topsoil will be arriving at seven A.M." I checked off bullet points in my head. "All right. I think we're done here. The excavation work is going to be—"

"Painful?" Deanna cut in.

That worked. The Lockhart yard was one of the most overgrown, weed-infested yards I'd ever seen. And I'd seen a lot of yards. I'd have turned the project down flat if I hadn't had ulterior motives for doing it. "Definitely. But once that's done, it should be clear sailing."

"You did it again," Tam called out from the reception area.

Aha! I'd known she was eavesdropping.

I peeked at her through the open door. She shook her finger at me.

"Is 'clear sailing' a cliché?" I asked.

Five heads bobbed.

I had picked up the worst habit of sounding like my mother, using abridged clichés and trite expressions. Except lately I'd noticed she'd been using them less and less, and I'd been using them more and more. "Hey! It wasn't abbreviated, though! That's something."

"It's hard to abbreviate a two-word cliché," Tam said, jotting something down. I imagined she had a notebook filled with my grammar transgressions.

Hmmph.

The small set of chimes attached to the front door rang out. The door used to have a cowbell, but the clanging had apparently gotten on Tam's nerves because I came in one day to find the bell flatter than a pan— I caught myself and stopped.

It was flat.

And there'd been a baseball bat nearby, namely in Tam's hands. I hadn't asked questions. The next day the chimes were on the door.

Heads craned to look out the conference room door to see who'd come in. Four sets of eyes then turned to me when Jean-Claude stumbled into the office.

"What?" I said to them.

"You need to take care of this." Kit rose.

I looked up, up, up at him. "I will."

He arched an eyebrow, and I noticed that he didn't look nearly as scary with a fuzzy head. It was hard to look scary with baby chicken hair.

I wondered if he knew that.

Didn't think I should be the one to tell him.

Jean-Claude froze when he spotted us. I *think* he spotted us, at least. Hard to say when he wore pitch-black Ray-Bans.

Everyone remaining at the table stood and scattered, leaving me to deal with Jean-Claude in private. "Come on in," I said to him.

"Was the meeting at eight? Thought it was at nine."

"Seeing as how it's almost ten, that's beside the point."

"You're mad."

I was. "Sit."

He slumped in Deanna's vacated chair, looking like Riley, my fifteen-year-old stepson, when he was in a mood.

In the reflection of his sunglasses I could see anger had darkened my already muddy green eyes. I noticed I needed a haircut too, my hair hanging past my shoulders. In my head it was easy to hear my sister Maria's voice telling me to go blonde like she was, but I was happy to be a brunette. For now.

I picked at the edge of a paper, folding it back and forth until it ripped. "What's going on?"

Taking off his sunglasses, he looked at me. I held back a gasp but could feel my eyes go wide, my anger dissipating into worry. Dark circles rimmed his eyes and streaks of red marred the white part around his dark pupils. "Overslept."

"You've been doing that a lot lately."

"I know. Sorry."

I jumped right in. "I think maybe it's time you found another job, Jean-Claude. Something nocturnal maybe."

His eyes grew wide, looking more bloodshot than before. "What?"

"I really can't have you working here anymore. Actually, you haven't been working much at all. The others have been covering for you for too long. And it's dangerous to have you working when you're so tired all the time. Some of the equipment—"

"Nina, please, you can't fire me."

My stomach hurt. "I really don't have a choice."

"I need the money," he said, leaning forward, over the table.

"*I* need *you* to work for the money."

"I will. Just give me another chance."

"Jean-Claude, this is about your hundredth chance."

"Please, Nina."

This all went back to me being a sucker for a sob story. I hated turning down someone in need. "Why do you need the money so badly?"

He pushed the heels of his hands into his eyes and rubbed. "Family trouble."

"Can you be more specific?"

"I'd rather not. It's embarrassing."

I looked out the conference room door, saw Tam sitting, listing left like a sinking boat, her ear cocked. She rarely missed much of what went on around here.

"You're not doing drugs are you?"

I heard a scraping noise from the wall behind me and had the feeling Kit, Deanna, Coby, and Marty were listening through the vent.

"What? No! I don't do that."

My eyebrow arched.

"Anymore," he put in.

The chimes on the front door startled me. My head snapped up.

She was here.

I gathered my files, stood up.

Jean-Claude glanced at me with big puppy dog eyes. "Please, Nina?"

Be strong, I told myself. "We'll talk about this later."

All right, so I copped out. But I really needed more information before I could fire him. Right?

Ugh.

I *hated* firing people.

As I walked out of the conference room, I heard scrambling from next door. I couldn't help but smile. At least I wasn't the only nosy one in the office.

"Lindsey," I said, holding out my hand to the tall winsome woman who'd just come in.

"Hi, Nina. Ready for me?" she asked as we shook.

I nodded as I led her into my office. Lindsey Lockhart.

Leah's sister.

Leah Quinn. Who happened to be Riley's mother. My soon-to-be-ex-husband Kevin's first wife.

The one who mysteriously died.

The one I knew nothing about.

Yet.

Two

I set the design board for the Lockharts' yard on an easel and sat in my swivel chair. "We just had our finalization meeting. Everything's on track."

"That's great," she said, her light eyes wide and bright as she stared at the board. "Everything looks just beautiful. I love those colors. The blues and whites are so soothing."

She had long brown hair, blonde highlights, and Riley's widow's peak. I wondered if her sister had had it too.

Leah Quinn had died long before I met Kevin, and in the eight years I'd been married to him, I'd never seen a single picture of the woman.

Riley must have her eyes. Kevin's were a dark green and Riley's were midnight blue.

"Thanks again for doing this, Nina. I know the yard is a mess."

An understatement if I'd ever heard one. The Lockhart yard . . .

I shuddered.

It was going to take a solid half day to excavate, even with Ignacio's crew's help. I made a mental note to confirm with Dexter Trucking that the extra dump trucks I hired would be at the site on time.

"When we—I mean I . . . When *I* found out through Riley about TBS, I couldn't believe my luck. It was just such perfect timing. I know it will be a tough job, though."

The "we" included Bill Lockhart, Lindsey's husband, who was the surprisee of this makeover.

"I'm always game for a challenge," I said. "Plus, we're practically family." When Riley had come to me, telling me that his aunt was interested in a makeover, I'd been fairly giddy. Finally, someone who knew the whole story about Leah's death.

When I saw the yard for the first time three weeks ago, I'd nearly backed out. My nosiness wasn't worth the trouble it was going to take to get the Lockhart job done in one day.

Then I'd thought of Riley. Of how happy he'd been lately. And I couldn't say no.

"How's Riley doing?" she asked.

"Pretty good. He really likes his job. Thanks for setting that up. He couldn't wait to get away from bagging groceries."

Lindsey laughed. "I don't know if flipping tofu burgers is a big step up, but Bill loves having him around."

Lindsey's husband Bill was the co-owner of Growl, a fast food restaurant featuring healthy alternatives. Riley had applied for a job there after one particularly horrifying afternoon at his old job as a grocery bagger when he'd been forced to triple bag someone's order; hit a car with a cart while on lot duty; and had his sneakers soaked in egg yolk when a plastic bag tore open, dumping out a carton of eggs. He'd quit that afternoon. It probably didn't help that he and his girlfriend Katie had broken up the night before.

He was still pouting over that, but it had been a month since he'd started his new job, and I hadn't heard a single complaint. Well, that wasn't true. Bill's business partner was apparently a micromanager, but after Riley learned that his uncle

Bill was in charge of the restaurant Mondays, Wednesdays, Fridays, and Saturday nights, he'd changed his schedule.

All had been peaceful in my household lately.

Which was somewhat disturbing.

My house was rarely peaceful.

Not with having a fifteen-year-old living with me. Plus, my divorce from Kevin was in its final stages. Oh, and let's not forget my dysfunctional family. Between Ana, my sister Maria, and my parents . . .

This was clearly the calm before the storm.

Lord help me.

"What kind of trees are these?" she asked.

"These two," I said, pointing, "are Bradford pears. Nice pear shape and beautiful white blossoms in the spring. This is an ash. Fairly quick grower, lots of shade, and pretty yellow gold foliage in the fall."

"It all looks so beautiful."

"Can I ask why you've let the yard go all these years?" I'd been dying to ask.

Her small upturned nose scrunched. "Honestly, it's just one of those things. Surely, you understand."

Not really. I couldn't imagine having what looked like a third world jungle for my backyard. But hey, that's me.

"I don't know if we'd be doing it at all if it weren't for the lawsuit."

I perked up, leaned over my stained desk blotter. "Lawsuit?"

"Neighborhood HOA. Homeowners' association."

My eyes went wide. "Really?"

"Really. The fines from not fixing the yard mounted and, well, Bill, he, um, is stubborn and, well . . . here I am."

My eyebrows twitched. Something didn't sound right.

Lindsey tsked. "Poor Greta."

"Greta?"

"Oh! Um, our dog."

"Your dog? What's that have to do with the lawsuit?"

She shifted in her chair. "I just meant that even without the lawsuit, it was past time to get the yard done. Greta barely has any room to move out there." Her hands fluttered. "Plus, the ticks. You know."

I fell back against my chair. My eyebrow started twitching again. My eyebrows were my secret weapon against load-of-bull stories. If the twitching was any indication, Lindsey was seriously shoveling me a line.

Why?

"Ticks," I repeated.

"All that long grass." Her head snapped to the design board. "Is that a fire pit?"

I noted the change of subject. "A ceramic one, yes. For the corner of the deck. We talked about that last time, if you remember."

"Oh, right. Right."

Something wacky was happening, but I didn't know what. Clearly flustered, Lindsey fidgeted in her seat and couldn't keep her hands still. Her eyes danced from me to the board to the floor and back again.

This might be the perfect time to get information out of her. "Have you and Bill been married long?"

She smiled. "Twelve years."

"Really? You don't look old enough to be married twelve years!"

I was such a liar. She looked forty if a day.

She blushed clear to the roots of her blonde highlights. "You're sweet. Thanks. I'm forty-three."

"Leah was your younger sister, then?"

A cloud passed over her eyes, and for a second I didn't

think she was going to answer me. Finally, she said, "Yes."

"It must have been hard."

"Hardest on Riley, I think," Lindsey murmured. "To lose his mom."

Kevin too, I figured. He'd grieved a long time for his first wife. Five years.

I put my hands in my lap, crossed my fingers. "What exactly happened to her?"

"Boating accident."

I knew that already. I pressed. "Did it crash?"

"Hasn't Kevin told you all this?"

Busted.

"Um, well, he doesn't like to talk about it."

"Neither do I, Nina. No offense."

This conversation was going downhill fast. "None taken," I said, thinking fast, grasping at straws.

I completely ignored my use of that particular cliché. It fit.

"It's just that since coming to work for you and Bill, Riley's been talking about his mom a lot. He has questions I can't answer."

I was going to burn in hell for my lies. I made a mental note to head to confession at St. Valentine's as soon as possible.

Then I remembered I hated confession.

Maybe I'd just do some acts of kindness on my own as penance. God would accept that, wouldn't He?

Probably I was going to hell.

"Have him come to talk to me. My door is always open."

To him. Her point was clear. She was done talking to *me* about it.

Great. I'd taken on this job to get more information about Leah and her death, and I'd just gotten shafted. Now I was stuck with a nightmare of a job and no answers.

This was what I got for snooping.

"Well, what's Bill doing tomorrow?" I loved hearing the ways people tricked unknowing spouses to leave the house while the makeover took place.

"Bill?" she asked, her eyebrows dipping in confusion.

"Oh, he'll be at work, right?" I remembered Riley worked tomorrow, a Friday, which meant it was a day Bill would be there.

"In the afternoon," she said.

My shoulders stiffened. "Not the morning?"

"Oh, no. The restaurant doesn't open till eleven. Bill likes to sleep late."

My crew was due to arrive at six-thirty, the trucks at seven. This wasn't good, and I told Lindsey so. "Unless he knows about the makeover?" Some people did that. People who just wanted their yard done in a day, but I tried to only take on clients who wanted the surprise, to keep the integrity of the business.

"Oh!" Her hands fluttered again. "Right. He's, um, going, um, fishing. First light."

My eyebrows jumped up to my hairline. "Fishing."

She nodded enthusiastically. "He loves it." Grabbing her purse, she said, "I've got to go, Nina. See you tomorrow."

I stood and walked her to the front door, all the while trying to make sense of what had just happened.

Frenzied chiming filled the air as she thrust open the door, practically ran to her Escalade.

I turned to Tam.

"You have that look," she said.

"What look?"

"Like you're trying to figure out impossible calculus equations."

Calculus. Ugh. I'd flunked that my senior year of high school and had only scraped by my freshman year of college.

And only then because I'd had a crush on my math tutor and wanted to please him.

"I get the weirdest feeling with her." The Escalade fishtailed out of the TBS parking lot.

"Like?" Tam asked.

"It's just that some of the things she's said don't jell. I don't know. Maybe I'm being paranoid."

"You are a paranoid kind of person."

"Thanks."

Smiling sweetly, she said, "No problem."

Shaking my head, I walked back into my office. The phone rang and my hopeful gaze jumped to the clock. Bobby usually called on his lunch break, at eleven-fifteen.

It was only ten-thirty.

Bobby MacKenna was Riley's vice principal during the school year. During the summer he helped out with his family's business—house painting. We'd been "dating" for almost six weeks now.

One of these days he was going to want to sleep with me.

Okay, okay. I needed to reword that. One of these days he was going to get sick of waiting for me to let him sleep with me.

I just hadn't been ready. How on earth could I let another man share my bed when I still had feelings for Kevin?

Homicide detective Kevin Quinn. Who in ten days would be my ex-husband.

Granted, I didn't quite know what those feelings were, but they were there. And until I figured them out, it wouldn't be fair to Bobby to pursue anything deeper, and it wouldn't be fair to me.

Then I thought about losing him, and my heart ached.

Jeez. A girl couldn't win.

"Nina?"

I turned and found Tam in the doorway, twisting her hands over her extended belly.

"What's the matter?" I asked. "The baby? Now?"

"No, no. I'm fine," she said, looking anything but.

My heart sank to my toes. "Then what?"

"There's been an accident. With Riley."

Three

White-knuckled, Tam clenched the steering wheel. "He's fine. Just fine. Everything's fine."

She drove because I was still shaking. My hands, my legs . . . Even my teeth chattered.

Riley.

Oh dear God. Please.

"Tell me again what Mr. Cabrera said?"

"Some sort of car accident, Nina. Riley was on his skateboard. He'll be fine. Just fine."

"Was he wearing his helmet?" I couldn't count the number of times I had to remind him to wear that helmet. He hated it. Called it "not cool."

Better not cool than dead, I'd told him.

Oh Lord, oh Lord.

Tam swerved out of the high-speed lane, into the center lane, and back into the left lane on I-275 eastbound. Horns honked in our wake. "I don't know." She pressed harder on the gas pedal.

"Oh no," she said.

"What?"

Then I heard it. The too familiar *whoop-whoop* of a police

car. I spun to look out the back window. Sure enough, a silver cruiser was right behind us.

Tam slowed and pulled off onto the berm. "Let me take care of this," she said, fluffing her curls.

Oh dear God.

With all the praying I was doing today, I definitely needed to visit St. Valentine's soon. Maybe I ought to make an appointment to see Father Keesler. I would need a while.

Tam's window slid down and she looked out at the officer peering in.

"Where's the fire?" he asked.

Original, I couldn't help but think sarcastically, but luckily kept my big mouth shut.

"Not fire, officer, water."

"Water?" he questioned.

"Mine broke! The baby's coming!" She motioned to her rather large belly. "I feel like I need to push!"

Tam was brilliant! I have excellent taste in employees. Then I remembered Jean-Claude. Okay, somewhat excellent taste.

"Yes," I said, "we really need to get to the hospital, officer."

He nodded to me. "Why aren't you driving?"

Why wasn't I?

"Oh," Tam said, "she's in no condition to drive."

"You been drinking, ma'am?"

Ma'am. Hmmph. "Me? No!"

"Painkillers," Tam whispered. "Back problems."

"Oh."

"Oooooh," Tam cried, holding her stomach.

"I'm going to call EMS," the officer said.

"No, no. I hate ambulances. I can make it . . . if we hurry."

The back of her head was to me, but I could imagine her blinking her beautiful blue eyes at him.

"Ma'am, I can't let you do that."

I lurched forward as Tam stepped on the gas. My jaw dropped open as I looked at her.

She smiled wide, a twinkle in her eye.

"You're insane!" I cried.

"Where's your sense of fun?" she asked, still grinning.

"Not here, that's for sure!" I peered around my headrest, looking out the back window. The officer had jumped in his car and was closing in fast. *Oh God.*

Sirens filled the air as he pulled in front of us, leading the way.

Tam said, "See?" and stepped on the gas.

"I didn't know you were such a good liar." I'd stopped shaking, but my heart was now beating in my throat.

"We all have our talents."

We made it to the hospital in less than five minutes. Tam parked the car under the emergency room portico and Officer Nice Guy helped her inside.

"Go, go," she told me, waving me off as a gurney appeared out of nowhere. The officer must have called ahead.

I ran up to the desk on wobbly legs. "Riley Quinn," I said.

The woman barely looked up. "And you are?"

"His mother," I lied. I didn't know if they'd let me in otherwise.

Behind the counter, she rolled her eyes. "Biggest family I ever saw. Go through those double doors, take a left at the green doors, a right through the red doors, then follow the blue line until you get to the nurses' station. Someone there will help you."

Green, red, blue, I repeated, trying to remember what she'd said as I pushed through the double doors.

My nose scrunched at the hated hospital smell. Not my favorite scent, that blend of antiseptic and illness.

A handrail lined one wall and a rainbow of colors decorated the floor. Looked like a class of preschoolers had had their way with a box of crayons.

I came to a set of yellow doors.

Yellow?

Red, green, blue. Green, red, blue? Blue, green, red?

No yellow at all! Oh no!

"Riley," I whispered loudly as I passed open doorways. What was it about hospitals and nursing homes? Why couldn't I pass a room without looking in? So far all I'd seen were two empty beds and a storage closet.

"Riley?" I whispered louder.

"Shhh!" someone said from within one of the rooms. "Trying to watch *Price Is Right!*"

"Sorry!"

I came to a set of green doors and decided to try my luck. I pushed through them. They led to another hallway that looked like it had a nurses' station at the end of it.

Quickly, I walked toward it, still unable to keep from peeping in the rooms I passed. I walked past an open door, looking in out of the corner of my eye, and stopped so fast I turned my ankle.

"Ow, ow, ow!" I hopped around like a rabid bunny. Not that I'd ever seen a rabid bunny, but I figured that's what I looked like.

I was rambling. Never a good sign.

"Nina Ceceri, is that you?"

Like nails on chalkboard, that voice, German accent and all. I thought about pretending to not hear her.

"I know you heard me," she snapped.

She sounded awfully healthy for someone lying in an E.R. hospital bed.

I backed up, stood in the doorway. "Mrs. Krauss, I really can't stay. I'm looking for Riley."

She sat upright, the oxygen tube in her nose straining. "Riley? Something's happened to the boy?"

The genuine fear in Brickhouse Krauss's eyes softened my hatred of her. "I don't know. I got a call that he'd been brought here."

She scrambled out of bed, tugging her johnnie around her to cover places I never ever wanted to see.

"I don't think that's a good idea," I said. "You're obviously not well."

A white eyebrow arched angrily. "Ach."

Ohh-kay.

With the oxygen tube abandoned and IV pole firmly in hand, Mrs. Krauss shuffled out the door, her paper-thin gown flapping.

"Did you check the nurses' station?" she asked me.

"No."

"Never were a good problem solver, were you, Nina Ceceri?"

Mrs. Krauss, aka Brickhouse Krauss, had been my English Lit teacher once upon a time. She was evil, pure and simple, but it seemed as though I was the only one who saw her that way. More recently she had an on-off relationship with my neighbor, Mr. Cabrera. Currently they were off, even though they really loved each other.

It was Mrs. Krauss's fear of dying that kept breaking them up. See, all Mr. Cabrera's lady friends had the unfortunate habit of kicking the bucket while dating him. Brickhouse freely admitted she broke up with him every few weeks to even the odds.

"Why are you here?" I asked her.

Her short white hair stuck out in wayward tufts. "I'm not dying, if that's what you're hoping."

"What? Me? Hoping? Never."

Again with the eyebrow as she narrowed her ice blue eyes on me. I shivered.

"So?"

"Pneumonia," she said. "Mild case."

The wheels on the IV pole squeaked as we walked down the hallway. "Isn't it funny that you get sick when you're *not* dating Mr. Cabrera? Didn't you get strep the last time you broke up with him? It's kind of ironic."

"What do you know about irony, Nina Ceceri?" she snapped.

"I paid *some* attention in your class."

"Hah!"

Thankfully, we'd reached the nurses' station, the center of four hallways that created an X. In an odd way, I was glad I'd run into Brickhouse. I had calmed down considerably. "Riley Quinn?" I asked the nurse on duty.

She checked a chart, said, "Room 5, down the hall on the right." She motioned straight ahead. "Follow the blue line."

As if it was that easy.

Brickhouse started in that direction, but I held back. "Tamara Oliver?" I asked.

Again with the chart flipping. "She's still being evaluated. Check back in a few minutes."

I said thanks and rushed to catch up to Brickhouse. As we neared Room 5, I could hear all sorts of commotion coming from within.

The first person I saw when I peeked in was Kevin. All the tears I'd been holding back welled in my eyes.

"Donatelli!" Mrs. Krauss said, clutching the front of her gown.

Everyone in the room turned to look at us in the doorway. My gaze skipped from Mr. Cabrera, who wore a pea-green-colored, short-sleeve button-down with a polar bear pattern, to an older woman with champagne-colored hair who I didn't recognize, to my cousin Ana, all big brown eyes, and finally to Kevin.

Kevin's gaze slammed into mine, and one of those dammed tears fell. "Where's Riley?" I asked, though it didn't sound like my voice at all, all choked and strained.

"Ursula!" I absently heard Mr. Cabrera say. "What are you doing here? Are you okay?"

In an instant Kevin was on his feet, headed toward me. I didn't even mind when he pulled me into a hug. "He's fine, Nina."

I could almost hear Tam's *I told you so.*

"Ach," Brickhouse said to Mr. Cabrera. "Like you care. Who's she?"

I heard the jealousy in her voice as Kevin's hand cupped the back of my head, his fingers gently kneading. He said, "A little accident."

I rested my forehead against his chest.

"A neighbor," Mr. Cabrera said. Out of the corner of my eye I saw his face turn three shades of purple. A neighbor, my foot. I didn't recognize the woman.

"I'm glad you're here," Kevin said.

How could he have betrayed me? How could he have walked away from seven pretty darn good years of marriage? For Ginger Ho. Er, Barlow. Ginger Barlow, his police partner.

I hated her.

And I remembered that I was supposed to hate him too.

I pulled back, out of his hug. Okay, it wasn't as fast as it could have been, but at least I did it.

Mind over matter and all that.

Oh no. There I went sounding like my mother again.

"Your mother's on her way," Ana said as if reading my mind. She came over, took my hand, held it tight. "Mr. Cabrera called her, and she called me. I was closer."

Half of Freedom probably knew about the accident by now, thanks to Mr. Cabrera's loose lips.

"Is Riley really okay?" I asked her, not wanting to look at Kevin. I had the uneasy feeling he knew I still loved him. That maybe, if he waged an all-out please-take-me-back war, I would. Take him back.

Would I?

Then what about Bobby? my inner voice asked.

I told it to please shut up.

That's me. Nina Colette Polite Ceceri Quinn.

"He's fine. He might have a broken wrist. He's in X-ray now."

"What happened?" I asked.

Mrs. Krauss was giving Mr. Cabrera's new girlfriend the evil eye. She did it quite well. My mother would be proud of her efforts.

Mr. Cabrera puffed out his chest. "Well, Miz Quinn, it's like this. Boom-Boom here—"

"Boom-Boom?" Brickhouse and I asked at the same time.

The older woman with sickly blonde hair stepped forward, smiled wide, her teeth as big and as yellow as the dingy locks on her head. I tried not to cringe.

"Boom-Boom Vhrooman," she said, holding out a hand. Reluctantly, I took it as she added, "I'm your new neighbor. I moved into Mrs. Warnicke's house."

"Ach."

"Now Ursula," Mr. Cabrera tried to soothe.

"Ach," she boomed.

He shut up.

Mrs. Warnicke had recently died of a heart attack after waking to find a burglar in her house. I wondered if Boom-Boom knew that. Some people might get spooked by living in a place where someone had recently died.

I knew I would.

Ana squeezed my hand. "Seems Boom-Boom and Riley had a head-on collision."

My gaze whipped to Kevin. He was sitting on Riley's empty bed and looked as though he were enjoying the play-by-play between Mr. Cabrera and Brickhouse. "And he only has a broken wrist?" I asked. "Are they sure?"

"Riley had his helmet on—"

Thank God.

"—and thankfully, Mrs. Vhrooman—"

"Boom-Boom, please," she cut in.

Kevin's mouth twitched. "*Boom-Boom* was driving a golf cart."

"It's actually not a golf cart," Boom-Boom supplied. "It's a motorized vehicle. Helps me get around. Bad heart, you know." She thumped her huge chest for emphasis.

I didn't think a woman with a bad heart should be hanging around Mr. Cabrera but kept that thought to myself. However, I noticed a small smile curved Mrs. Krauss's lips. Apparently she'd had the same thought and was pleased by her conclusion.

A kind-looking nurse stuck her head through the doorway. She was awfully pretty, with long, slightly curly hair, big brown eyes, and a warm smile. Her name badge read MEGAN LITTLE, RN. I checked to see if Kevin was checking her out.

He wasn't.

It made me feel marginally better.

"Mrs. Krauss," Megan Little, RN, said, "there you are. Your daughter is worried sick trying to find you. Come with me."

Brickhouse looked like she was going to argue, but just arched an eyebrow at Mr. Cabrera, turned, and dragged her IV pole out the door.

"Is she really sick?" Mr. Cabrera asked me. "There is that nasty flu bug going around."

"She'll be fine." No one that mean could stay down long. "You could go be with her," I suggested.

Boom-Boom pouted.

Mr. Cabrera shook his head. "Nah. She broke up with me. I'm not gonna go crawlin' back."

I silently added *Again.* Honestly, he had put up with a lot from her. Though I had to admit, I'd never seen him happier than when he was with her.

And she did have a somewhat valid reason for breaking up with him. I couldn't imagine it was easy to live with certain death hanging over your head.

Someone coughed from the doorway. I turned and saw a handsome man, early forties, big blue eyes, bright white teeth, standing there wearing a lab coat. A stethoscope hung around his neck. Ana perked up.

"Doctor," she said, abandoning my hand to rush over to him, "is Riley okay?"

"Coming through," someone said from the hallway.

Ana and Dr. Feelgood parted, allowing Riley, being pushed in a wheelchair, to enter. He hopped out of the wheelchair and onto the edge of the bed, his legs swinging.

The doctor patted Ana's hand and smiled at her. "Fine. The X rays showed no breaks at all." He looked at Riley. "With a sprain this severe, however, it's best you keep it easy for a few days. No skateboarding."

Riley's dark blue eyes went wide. "What about work?"

"What do you do?" Dr. Feelgood asked him.

"I work at Growl. Sometimes the register, sometimes with food prep."

The doctor bit his lip, and I couldn't help but roll my eyes at how Ana stared at him.

"It would be best to take a day or two off. The nurse has some paperwork for you, but after that you all are free to go."

We thanked Dr. Feelgood, and he turned to leave. It was no surprise to see Ana follow him out. Even though she'd been dating riverboat security guard S. Larue—we still didn't know his first name—off and on for a solid month now, she was always on the prowl.

"I can't miss work," Riley said to Kevin.

"They'll understand."

Riley scowled. He was a good scowler. "Ebenezer won't."

"Ebenezer?" I asked.

Mr. Cabrera said, "Russ Grabinsky." At my confused look, he added, "Riley's boss."

I stared. I didn't even want to know how Mr. Cabrera knew the man's name when I didn't.

"He'll fire me now for sure," Riley said. "He doesn't like me."

"Your uncle Bill won't let that happen," Kevin said, clapping Riley on the back. "I'll call him tonight."

It amazed me how the two of them looked so much alike. Both tall, dark, and brooding.

"I can call him," Riley said.

It still shocked me when Riley showed signs of maturity. One of these days I was going to have to get used to it.

"No hard feelings?" Boom-Boom asked Riley.

"Nah," he said. "Come into Growl sometime. Dinner is on me."

Boom-Boom beamed and patted his cheek.

Hmmph. He never let *me* pat his cheek.

Megan Little, RN, poked her head in again. "Nina Quinn?" she asked.

"That's me," I said, slightly confused.

"Tam Oliver is asking to see you. If you could follow me?"

Tam! I'd forgotten about Tam. I could only imagine the superfluous tests they were subjecting her to.

"I'll be right back," I told Riley.

Kevin's brows creased in worry. "Is Tam okay?"

I thought about her Oscarworthy performance in the car. "She's fine."

I followed the nurse down the red-lined hallway and stopped in my tracks when I stepped into Tam's room. She was hooked up to all sorts of monitors, including one tortuous looking belt-thingy wrapped around her stomach.

The nurse said to Tam, "I contacted Mr. Phillips. He's on his way." She closed the door behind her.

"Ian? Ian's coming here?" I asked.

The father of Tam's baby was her first husband, a marriage that had been declared null and void after she discovered he already had a wife. He'd been in jail when Tam found out she was pregnant, and I didn't know if he knew about the baby. Knowing Tam, probably not. And since he'd be serving time for a few more years, I wondered if he'd *ever* know about the baby.

But if Ian was coming, something serious must be wrong. He and Tam had been dating hot and heavy for about a month now. Were head over heels despite the fact that Ian was an FBI agent and Tam had a thing against people who wore badges. I rushed over to the bed. "Tam, what's wrong?"

She sniffled. "How's Riley?"

"Fine. Just fine."

A grin spread across her face. "I told you so."

I smiled in spite of the knot of worry twisting my stomach. "What's wrong?"

"I have to stay here."

"What! Why?"

"It seems I'm not such a good liar after all. I'm having contractions. Looks like the baby wants to come early."

Four

I'd barely slept at all last night between worrying about Tam and trying to figure out what I was going to do without her at TBS.

Shading my eyes against the early morning sun, I surveyed the Lockharts' backyard and wondered if it was too early to call the hospital.

All my other calls had resulted in the same outcome: No change in Ms. Oliver's condition.

A truck rumbled in the distance. I hoped it was Kit with the skid loader. The yard was going to take a while to clear out, but luckily the first dump truck had arrived on time, so we were all ready to begin when Kit showed.

The doctors put Tam on some sort of medication to stop the contractions until they had time to give her steroids to help the baby's lungs develop.

She could be in the hospital for days, possibly weeks.

I just prayed that the baby would be okay.

"Nina, you're here!" Lindsey said. "This is so exciting."

Even with my Tam worries, I was excited too. I loved the buzz of the actual makeover day. The adrenaline, the challenges, the fast pace. This yard would definitely be a challenge, but the end result would be a job well done.

Bright sunshine highlighted every flaw of the yard. Thank God the Lockharts had finally called someone for help, even though it had taken a lawsuit to provoke them. I looked at Lindsey. "Bill make it out okay this morning?"

"What? Oh! The fishing. Yes, yes."

I noticed she wrung her hands. My eyebrow quivered. What was going on? "Is there anything you need to tell me?"

"What? No. Nothing at all."

Overall, I loved surprises. It's one of the reasons I loved my job so much. However, I didn't like feeling as though Lindsey was keeping something from me. Especially if it might be something that put my reputation or company at risk.

"There's a big truck out front towing a trailer with a Bobcat on it," she said.

That had to be Kit. "We'll be using the skid loader most of the morning, clearing all this out." I gestured to the quarter acre of overgrown grass and weeds and a couple of rotting trees. (Okay, I have to admit I was pleasantly surprised to not find a rusting car resting on four cinder blocks amidst the weeds. Yes, it was that bad.)

I looked to my left, over a small picket fence. The house next door had a beautifully kept lawn, a trimmed boxwood hedge, nice planting beds, and an adorable little greenhouse.

To my right, the neighbor's yard was enclosed with a six-foot wrought-iron fence. Tall fountain grasses provided privacy all along its perimeter. There was no seeing in, and no seeing out.

It was easy to imagine why. No one wanted to view the Lockharts' yard in its current state. Not even me.

"Does the HOA know about the work going on here today?" I'd had issues with homeowner associations before and didn't want to deal with that kind of hassle today.

Lindsey shook her head. "No."

"Are they going to be up in arms over it? We'll be making a lot of noise."

"They want the yard fixed up more than anyone."

I just hoped there wouldn't be any problems. My stress level couldn't take any more.

"I'm going to, uh, go grocery shopping," she said, already stepping away. "You have my cell phone number?"

Again my eyebrow twitched. Something just wasn't right about this whole job. Most clients liked to stick around, watch our progress. Some even baked us cookies and brought us lemonade. I was bummed. I'd wanted a chance to poke around her house, see if there were any pictures of Leah Quinn lying around. "Yes."

"What time will you be done?" she asked, looking somewhat worried.

Both eyebrows lifted. Uh-oh. Something was definitely wrong. "Six."

"Right. Six. Okay. 'Bye!"

I heard Kit unloading the skid loader and went down to the curb to see if Jean-Claude had showed.

He hadn't.

I growled.

That was it. He was so fired when I saw him.

No more Ms. Nice Guy.

Girl.

Whatever.

There I went again, rambling to myself. Never a good sign my day was going to go well.

I decided to make myself useful as Kit tackled the backyard with the help of Ignacio and his crew.

To help ease my tension, I decided to get started with the planters. Nothing soothed me more than planting flowers, getting my hands dirty. I dumped my clipboard into the cab of my TBS truck and made sure my cell phone was clipped to my waistband.

The only color in the front yard was a terra cotta pot full of thriving white pansies on the front step. Maybe if there were leftover flowers from the backyard, I'd have Deanna add some to the front mulch bed, where three sad-looking spireas were in need of pruning.

From the bed of the truck I pulled out five large glazed white pots and set each on the ground. They were tall, maybe two and a half feet high, but not very wide. Maybe eighteen inches at best.

I hunted around the utility truck for gravel, which would provide good drainage and stability, and for potting soil, which I would mix with topsoil for planting.

I'd just finished stacking five sacks of potting soil on the Lockharts' driveway when a hoity-toity female voice said from behind me, "Who are you?"

I turned. A small woman with long blonde hair stood on the curb, eyeing me.

"Nina Quinn," I said. I held out a hand to shake, but caught a glimpse of it. Filthy. I rarely used gloves when planting. I pulled my hand back. "And you are?"

"Meredith Adams."

That cleared that up.

Under severely plucked eyebrows big blue-gray eyes bulged slightly. Why they bulged I had no idea. Was this some sort of evil eye I'd never encountered?

When she continued to stare, I began wondering if she was all there. Upstairs.

"What are you doing here?" she finally said on an exasperated sigh, and I realized she'd been waiting for an explanation. That cleared up the eye-flaring thing.

Unfortunately, I had issues with people interrogating me

for no apparent reason. "What are *you* doing here?" I asked her. Ha! Take that.

"I asked first."

"So?"

"So? So answer!"

It was wrong toying with her like this, but I couldn't help myself. Not with the way she stood there, five feet of quivering righteous indignation. "You."

She drew in a deep breath, held it, and then released it in a snorty way, like a bull before it charged. "I am Meredith Adams, vice president of Fallow Falls Homeowners Association. I demand to know what is going on."

I just couldn't help myself. I blamed it on the stress of my day. "Sorry. I only speak to presidents." I lifted a bag of potting soil and shrugged.

She turned from valentine pink to fire engine red in two seconds flat. Her mouth opened widely, then closed again with an audible click. Pencil thin pale eyebrows dipped dangerously low as she tried hard for an evil eye. With the slight bulge, she just couldn't pull it off.

I bit my lip hard to keep from laughing.

"Uhhnn!" she squawked, spinning on her Ann Taylor wedges. Fists pumped as she speed-walked down the sidewalk.

I was definitely going to hell.

My mood lifted, I turned, potting soil in hand. "Eee!" I screamed as a big black blur barreled down on me.

"Nina, look out!" someone yelled unnecessarily.

I didn't even have time to brace myself before two enormous paws landed on my shoulders and pushed me backward. I tripped on the stack of potting soil sacks and fell down on the grass.

Pain radiated from my, er, backside. The sacks of soil I'd already stacked stopped my head from hitting the cement.

Bits of soil flew everywhere as claws tore into the bag I still held onto. For dear life.

A huge tongue assaulted me, licking my face up and down, side to side.

I knew that tongue.

BeBe. Kit's dog.

"Get her off me!" I cried, trying not to open my mouth. Drool oozed down my face. Ewww! "BeBe, down! Down!"

This was some sort of cosmic justice, I just knew it.

A sharp whistle pierced the air. BeBe immediately retreated and began prancing around, her tongue lolling out of the corner of her mouth. She pranced rather gracefully for an enormous 150-pound, wrinkly-faced, drooling English mastiff.

Dazed, I glanced up. Kit's goofy grin split his whole face. "She missed you," he said.

Lifting my head, I saw that Jean-Claude stood behind Kit, a leash in his hands. He shrugged. "Sorry. She got away from me."

"What's BeBe doing with you?" I sputtered, still confused.

"Kit had me babysitting her."

Kit snatched the leash out of Jean-Claude's hands. "Lot of good it did me." He attached a hook to BeBe's collar.

"Well you didn't tell me she'd freak out when she saw Nina." Jean-Claude gestured to my prone body.

Tiredly, I asked, "What's BeBe doing *here*?"

BeBe lunged toward me when she heard her name. Kit's muscles bulged as he held her back. "Daisy got an emergency call and had to drop her off."

Daisy? I craned my neck to see down the street. "Daisy was here?"

"Thirty minutes ago," Jean-Claude said.

"What? You saw her?"

"She's not a ghost," Kit snapped.

"Actually, I didn't see *her*." Jean-Claude scratched his eight A.M. shadow. "I just saw the car driving away. It's a sweet ride."

Damn. I'd missed her!

"You better not be looking at her ride," Kit warned, his eyes dark.

Jean-Claude had a history of stealing cars in his youth. I wasn't so sure he'd given up the pastime. Not with his weird behavior lately.

Jean-Claude held up his hands, palms out. "What ride?"

Kit nodded.

My butt ached. I groaned and accepted Jean-Claude's hand to help me up.

BeBe strained at her leash to get back to me. "Why bring her here? Why not leave her at home?"

Kit's eyes widened. "By herself?"

"Yeah?"

"That's harsh, Nina. She's just a baby."

A hundred-and-fifty-pound baby.

"She's a dog."

Kit's face contorted in disbelief.

"Fine, fine," I said, giving in. "Just keep her out of the yard and get back to work."

"What am I supposed to do with her?"

I gave him a how-am-I-supposed-to-know look.

Jean-Claude cleared his throat. "I'll watch her."

My jaw dropped open. "Hello? You work for *me*. Besides, look what happened last time you watched her."

"She was just excited to see you," he said. "I wasn't prepared for it. Now I am."

Kit rubbed BeBe's ears. They flopped back and forth. "He has a point. And if he doesn't watch over her, I'm going to have to run her over to my mom's."

"Your mom lives in Lima." Four hours away round-trip.

"Exactly."

"Fine," I said, looking between the two of them. "But if I need your help, Jean-Claude, BeBe goes in the truck with the AC on. Got it?"

"Yes, ma'am."

Hmmph. Ma'am. That was twice this week. It made me want to fire him more than his recent misbehavior.

"Kit?" I asked.

"All right." He handed BeBe off to Jean-Claude, who wrapped the leash around his wrist three times and started off down the street.

Kit looked at me. "Home alone? C'mon, Nina."

"She's a dog!"

With a disgusted look, he turned and headed into the backyard.

Stanley Mack, the carpenter I contracted, drove up the street, a load of lumber in the back of his truck. I waved.

I managed to work for four hours straight without any other interruptions. It was almost eleven-thirty when someone tapped me on the shoulder. "Nina Quinn?"

The woman backed up a step when I turned. I wondered if it had anything to do with me being covered in dirt. "Yes?"

"I'm Kate Hathaway. President of the Fallow Falls Homeowners Association."

She was awfully pretty, with big blue eyes and reddish-blonde hair. "Ah. Meredith sent you."

"Meredith is a bit high-strung." She smiled, showing no teeth, yet it still seemed genuine. "But she means well."

I wasn't so sure. Not about the high-strung part—she definitely was—but about the meaning well part. I thought she rather enjoyed being bossy and demanding.

When I didn't say anything, she went on. "I just need to make sure you have all the proper permits."

I'd dealt with HOAs before, so I knew the drill. "They're over here," I said, walking her to my truck. The little ankle bracelet she wore tinkled as we walked, reminding me of TBS's chimes, which reminded me of Tam, which reminded me I hadn't called her in the last thirty minutes to see if she was okay.

It would have to wait until I was done with Madame President.

I grabbed my clipboard and the folder where I kept important files. I was rooting through it when she said, "Does Greta know about this?"

"Greta?" I asked. The Lockharts' dog?

"She's rather particular."

My hand stilled. "The dog?"

"What dog?"

"Greta?"

Her big blue eyes got even bigger. "Greta's not—"

"Nina!" Jean-Claude yelled. "Help!"

In a blink I took it all in. The big black dog chasing the small white cat. The dog-sitter spread-eagle on the sidewalk, holding his wrist.

I dropped my papers and took off running after BeBe, who'd already disappeared into the backyard.

"BeBe," I yelled. "Here, BeBe!"

"BeBe!" Jean-Claude had picked himself up and was running alongside me. He turned worried eyes to me. "Is Kit going to kill me?"

"Yes."

He slowed down. "Maybe I should go."

I grabbed his arm, tugged him along. "Not until you catch her!"

"BeBe!" he yelled.

She wouldn't even look at us. Her focus was completely on the little cat who seemed to be enjoying running BeBe ragged.

The skid loader's engine fell silent. "Oh no," Jean-Claude murmured.

"BeBe! Come to Nina!" I urged. No luck. She galloped through the backyard, this way and that.

"Jean-Claude!" Kit bellowed.

Jean-Claude went pale.

"Maybe you ought to go after all," I said.

He turned and ran.

The cat dashed into the woods behind the house. BeBe followed it. I followed her.

Kit whistled, but BeBe wasn't listening. "What happened?" he yelled to me.

I thought it was fairly obvious, so I didn't answer.

The shady woods were full and thick with greenery. Everything from honeysuckle vines to squishy mushrooms covered the ground. Breathing hard, I hopped over a small creek and was relieved to see BeBe circling a large buckeye tree.

I bent at the waist, drawing in oxygen.

Kit powered through the woods and grabbed hold of BeBe's leash. He looked at me. "Time for a trip to the gym?"

"Ha." Gasp. "Ha."

BeBe apparently noticed my presence for the first time because she ran over and slobbered my face. "Eww!"

"She just loves you."

I shot Kit a look.

"Nina!" Coby yelled from the edge of the woods.

I walked toward him, noticing he looked a bit piqued. "What's wrong?"

He pointed to an older man standing near the house. "He wants to talk to you."

I didn't recognize him. I just hoped he wasn't another homeowners' official. Using the back of my hand, I wiped the sweat from my forehead, the drool from my face, and hurried down the hill.

I noticed two things right off. The man held a Growl take-out bag in his hand (it's hard to miss being all black with bright yellow lettering), and he didn't look well at all. He was shouting at Marty.

"What is going on here? This is private property!" Sweat beaded on his brow. "Who are you people? No one gave permission for this!"

My lungs burned. Maybe a trip to the gym wasn't such a bad idea. Pulling in a shallow breath, I said, "I'll take care of this, Marty."

Next, I tried for a soothing tone. "Sir, calm down."

The take-out bag crinkled in his closed fist. "Don't tell me to calm down, little lady. This is America. I can be as *not* calm as I want! Where's my wife?"

Little lady. Hmm. I couldn't decide whether this insult was a step up or step down from "ma'am."

Kit snorted from behind me. I turned and gave him the evil eye. Even BeBe ducked behind Kit's legs.

The man stomped across the cracked cement patio, threw open the back door of the house, and disappeared inside. The house I was quickly suspecting did not belong to the Lockharts.

I felt sick.

"Greta!" he yelled, his voice thunderous.

Uh-oh. Was he yelling for his dog . . . or his wife?

I felt *really* sick.

He came back out a second later without the take-out bag, both fists clenched tight, like he was ready to take a swing. Sweat dripped from his receding hairline. He looked hot yet cold at the same time. Sweating yet pale.

Stepping back, I wondered if I had any degerminator in my truck. The man obviously had the flu or something.

He bellowed, "I come home from work not feeling well, just wanting some rest, relaxation, and a little soup, and this is what I find! People desecrating my yard! What is going on?" Color sat high on his hollow cheekbones, standing out against his pale skin.

"Surprise!" I said. "I'm Nina Quinn, owner of Taken by Surprise, Garden Designs. I was hired to makeover this backyard."

"Hired! By who?"

I didn't think this was the time to correct his grammar. I gulped. I'd been hired by Lindsey Lockhart to surprise her husband.

This clearly was not Bill. I'd met him many times picking Riley up from work. So either Lindsey was a polygamist or I'd been tricked. It was a sticky situation. I didn't know what to do, what to say, and I hated that I'd been put in this position.

"Um, the homeowner?" I asked, hoping against hope that I was wrong about this house belonging to this man.

"Are you toying with me, little lady?"

Again the snort from Kit. What on earth was going on? I expected *Candid Camera* any second.

"*I* am the home—" He broke off mid-word, his eyes widening. He clutched his chest, his lips parting in a silent scream. His knees buckled and he toppled over. He landed in a motionless heap at my feet.

Five

Kit immediately handed me BeBe's leash and started CPR. I watched him do chest compressions, stopping to breathe air into the man's lungs every so often.

"He's dead!" a voice over my shoulder said.

It was Meredith Adams, HOA VP, her eyes on bulge overload.

"No, he's not," I said, hoping it was true. *Please God, let it be true.* I swore right then and there I'd go to confession every week for the rest of my life if it were true.

"Yes, he is. You killed him!"

"Did not!"

"Did too."

"Go away!"

Someone grabbed Meredith's arm and tugged. It was Kate Hathaway. I gave her a grateful smile.

Kit pressed and breathed.

Dear God. I'd never had someone die at one of my sites. BeBe, probably sensing something important was going on, sat at my feet, content to lick my hand. I didn't even mind. All I kept thinking about was what the man had said. Or what he'd been about to say. I *am the homeowner.*

This man was clearly *not* Bill Lockhart.

Who the hell was he?

I turned to Madame President to ask, but she and Meredith Adams were gone. Marty and Coby stood huddled by the neighbor's picket fence, their eyes wide with disbelief. Ignacio and his crew had disappeared. I didn't blame them. In a few minutes this place would be crawling with officials. Officials who might think to check green cards.

Sirens rang in the distance.

They'd gotten here fast, though I rather suspected it was too late for the man. John Doe's face had turned a pale shade of blue, his lips a plum color. And his eyes . . . I shuddered. They were open wide but not seeing a thing.

Still, Kit worked on him. The man had clearly been ill, and I wondered if he was contagious as Kit did mouth-to-mouth.

I looked down the hill to the sidewalk and saw an ambulance pull up diagonally at the curb. As the paramedics rushed toward us, they brought a crowd of onlookers. BeBe excitedly danced around my feet at all the new faces.

When she tried to help Kit with the CPR by licking John Doe's face, I tugged sharply on her leash and led her to my truck.

I rolled down the windows two inches, turned on the AC, and called Lindsey Lockhart's cell phone.

No one answered.

A police cruiser pulled up behind the ambulance. A uniformed officer got out and hurried up the slope into the backyard.

Still no answer when I tried Lindsey's cell again. I left a message.

I figured the cop would want to ask me questions, so I left BeBe drooling on my gear shift and listening to the Oldies station. Kit stood with folded arms on the fringe of the crowd. The paramedics still worked on John Doe, using a portable defibrillator.

Everyone stood in silence, just watching.

After twenty minutes of futile effort one of the paramedics made a phone call. After he hung up, he and his partner started putting away their gear.

Out of nowhere a sheet appeared, and they draped it over the man's face and shoulders, leaving his arms and legs sticking out, like some sort of off-kilter stick figure.

I turned away.

Several officers now swarmed the yard, clearing people out. Kit had disappeared. I assumed he was off coddling BeBe. Marty, Coby, and Stanley Mack had moved to the shade under the eaves of the house.

People began speaking as they walked away, softly at first, but then more loudly. I was able to pick out pieces of conversation.

I didn't like him, but I'd never wish this on him.

Hasn't seen his kid in ten years.

A bastard to work with too.

The way he treated Greta . . . the man should have been in jail.

Neighborhood will be better now that he's gone.

I heard his wife was hoping he'd have a heart attack when he saw the yard. That's why she hired these people.

Rumors flew. I wanted to yell that this man's wife hadn't hired me at all. Lindsey Lockhart had. To surprise her husband Bill.

But the man on the ground wasn't Bill. And this yard apparently wasn't the Lockharts'.

Lindsey had lied to me.

I tapped someone on the shoulder. The man turned, his light blue eyes narrowing. I said, "Do you happen to know this man's name?"

"Russ Grabinsky," he said. "The lowest form of scum that ever lived."

Ohh-kay. "And he lived here?" I asked, double-checking.

"For over thirty years."

"Where, ah, do the Lockharts live?"

The man hooked a thumb over his shoulder at the house next door, the one with the cute picket fence and greenhouse. "There. Why?"

"No reason."

We both looked back at the covered body.

"I'm glad he's dead," he said, then stalked off, stopping to speak with Kate Hathaway for a brief moment before storming down the hill.

I forced my mouth closed. It's one thing not to like a man, but another to say you're glad he's dead.

My gaze went back to the body on the ground.

Russ Grabinsky. Grabinsky. I'd heard the name before, but I couldn't place it. It had been recent too.

I cursed getting older just as a uniformed officer came over to me. "Hello, Nina."

"Hey, Davis." The Freedom Police Department was very close-knit. Everyone knew everyone. I wondered how long it would take for this incident to get back to Kevin.

"Bad day, huh?" Davis asked, tapping his small notebook.

I bit back any sarcastic comments. No need to antagonize. "I've had better."

"Just need to ask a few questions."

I nodded.

"Who hired you?"

"Lindsey Lockhart."

"She here?"

I looked around, didn't see her traitorous self anywhere. I'd known something was off about this job. Dammit. When was I going to listen to my instincts? "No."

"She live here?"

"I guess not," I said, unable to completely cover my sarcasm.

"Did you have the homeowner's permission to work this land?"

"Apparently not." I eyed my fingernails, in need of biting one, but they were just too dirty. I crossed my arms instead.

Davis whistled low.

Just then a woman came waddling quickly up the hill, her face flushed with exertion. She was older, maybe mid-sixties, with an old-fashioned beehive hairdo. She wore an old housecoat with faux pearl buttons. "Russell!" she cried when she spotted the sheet-covered body on the ground.

"Greta!" Kate Hathaway rushed over to her, put an arm around the woman's broad shoulders.

Davis said, "I'll be right back."

So this was Greta. Not a dog after all. I looked around for Lindsey Lockhart, thinking there might be two deaths today.

I moseyed over to stand with the guys while the police and the homeowners' association welcome wagon filled Mrs. Grabinsky in.

I recalled what one of the passersby had said about her wanting to kill her husband and wondered why people would think so. Had their marriage been bad? Had he been abusive? Was she glad he was gone?

She certainly wasn't acting glad. Tears flowed.

Crocodile tears?

"No, no, no!" she cried as one of the paramedics asked her which mortuary to call. "I want an autopsy done!"

Why? I wondered.

"Why?" the paramedic asked, bless him.

"Because I want to know why he died. My Russell was a healthy man. This just does not happen to healthy men!"

"You know that's not true, Greta," a voice from behind me said.

Lindsey. When had she shown up? Had she been hiding nearby all along? I glared at her, but she wouldn't look at me, so I supposed it had little effect.

"What's not true?" Davis asked, stepping into the conversation.

Lindsey clasped her hands together. "Russell wasn't that healthy."

Mrs. Grabinsky's eyes narrowed.

"You know he wasn't, Greta. He was taking high blood pressure medication. You told me so yourself."

Russ Grabinsky. Ebenezer! Of course. That's where I'd heard the name. Yesterday at the hospital. Russ Grabinsky was the Growl co-owner Riley despised.

Greta put her meaty hands on her meatier hips. "Nothing that would cause this!"

"Actually," the paramedic said, "high blood pressure could cause a heart infarction."

The vicious glare turned to him. He looked at Davis.

"If there's any suspicion at all, an autopsy must be done."

The paramedic looked like he wanted to argue, but said, "We'll transport the body to the coroner's office, then."

Davis nodded, jotted something in his notebook.

Everyone watched silently as Russ Grabinsky was loaded onto a gurney, the white sheet still covering him, and rolled down the hill into a waiting van.

Wild-eyed, Greta backed away from us, her hands shaking. She pointed to Lindsey. "This is your fault! You had no right, not at all, to do this."

Lindsey pleaded, "Greta, be reasonable. I was trying to help you."

"Help? Ha! By sending my husband to an early grave?"

"Greta—"

"You'll be hearing from my lawyer!" Greta cried.

Hmmph. I had a visit to my lawyers in mind as well, to deal with Lindsey.

"And you!" A craggy finger shook at me.

"Me?"

"You will pay too."

I gasped. "What did I do?"

"You murdered my husband."

Murmurs rippled through the yard.

"As far as I'm concerned it was your unauthorized work here that caused his heart attack. You will pay, little lady."

The use of "little lady" barely even registered. All I could think of was how I was going to deal with this. Because Greta Grabinsky actually had a good case against me.

Not about the murder, of course. That was ridiculous. But about the unauthorized work. Technically, I'd destroyed her property. She could sue me for everything I had.

I could lose everything.

Six

An hour later I stood staring at the mess in the backyard. Most of the clearing had been done, at least.

"You know, you need to finish this job ASAP."

Meredith Adams's voice worked my last nerve. "Why's that?"

"You cannot leave this yard in the state it's in. It's an eyesore. A blight on the neighborhood."

"Is it?"

"Yes, it is."

"Will you sue me?" I asked, my voice low.

She took a step back, out of range of my hand, which was itching to smack her.

She tossed her long hair over her shoulder. She looked about my age, maybe a little older. "Besides, the work has been paid for. *You've* been paid. It's only right you finish the job."

I didn't feel like explaining that I couldn't finish the job until I had the homeowner's permission. And judging by Greta's current state, I didn't think that was going to happen anytime soon.

A deep masculine voice said, "That's not going to happen. At least not today."

My stomach muscles clenched. I turned to find Kevin standing there, a speculative glint in his green eyes.

"What's with you and dead bodies?" he asked.

Meredith gasped. "You mean there's been more than one?"

I fisted my hands and tucked them under my armpits so I wouldn't deck Little Miss Sunshine and Light.

"None of them were my fault," I said, feeling defensive, especially when Meredith gasped again.

"That remains to be determined."

Uh-oh. "What are you doing here?" I asked. Kevin was a homicide detective. He, well, detected homicides. Which this wasn't. This was a heart attack.

"Davis called about a suspicious death."

"It's not suspicious. He had a heart attack."

"Is it considered a heart attack if the victim is shocked to death?" Meredith piped in. "Because Russ Grabinsky was shocked by his backyard. Keeled right over when he saw it."

I backed up a step so I wouldn't kick her. "It wasn't right over," I argued. "He went inside and everything before he came back out—"

"And keeled over," Meredith said.

"Who are you?" Kevin asked.

"Meredith Adams. I'm the vice president of the Fallow Falls Homeowners Association."

Kevin pulled out his notebook. I didn't know why. He never actually wrote anything down. He'd had that same notebook for four years. "And you knew the victim?"

Out of the corner of my eye I saw Ginger Ho, er, Barlow coming up the slope along the side of the house. She stopped to look at the spot where Russ Grabinsky had died.

Great. My day just kept getting better and better.

Meredith's expression soured. "Everyone knew Russ."

"Everyone hated Russ," I supplied.

Both of them looked at me. "Oh, come on," I said. "One guy told me he was glad Russ was dead."

Kevin's eyebrow jumped. "I'll need that name."

"I don't know it. Though I did see him speak to Kate Hathaway, the Fallow Falls Homeowners Association *president,* before he left. Tall guy, Nordic looking, blond, amazing cheekbones, light blue eyes."

Kevin's other eyebrow dipped. "Amazing cheekbones?"

"Well, it's hard not to notice them."

"Do you think *you* should be noticing them? What would your Ken doll think?"

Kevin had issues with Bobby, obviously. Issues he had no right to whatsoever. I gritted my teeth, spoke softly through them. "Probably the same thing Ginger would think if she knew you kissed me a month ago."

Now his eyebrows waggled. "Still thinking about that, are you?"

Argh!

"Do you two know each other?" Meredith asked, confusion creasing the faint wrinkles on her forehead and pulling down the corners of her mouth.

"She's my wife," Kevin said.

"Almost ex," I pointed out.

The divorce would be final in nine days.

Nine days.

My stomach hurt.

"Isn't this a conflict of interest?" Meredith asked.

"No," Kevin and I both said at once.

"Who's Kate Hathaway?" he asked.

I filled him in.

"And the Nordic guy is her husband Dale." Color rose up Meredith's neck. "And he does have amazing cheekbones."

I shot Kevin an I-told-you-so look.

He ignored it. "Did Dale and Russ Grabinsky get along?"

Meredith fidgeted. "I don't like to talk."

Right.

"This is an official investigation," Kevin told her. "You have to talk."

It seemed to me all Meredith wanted was a little prodding. "Well, no. They didn't get along. They hated each other."

"Why?"

"It's complicated. The Hathaways live there," she said, pointing right next door to the house with the wrought-iron fence and fountain grasses. "There's always been animosity between them. The Hathaways wanted to move about two years ago and quickly found out that not only had their house depreciated in value because of the Grabinskys' yard, but also no one would buy it because of the eyesore. It was on the market for almost ten months. Finally they gave up and formed the homeowners' association."

Ah. To get the Grabinskys to comply.

"Russ was mad that Greta had joined the association, but I think she really wanted the yard done and thought that would spur him to do it."

"Why didn't Russ just fix the yard?" I asked.

Meredith shrugged. "He was a jerk. I don't even know why Greta stayed with him. Anyway, Russ refused to fix the yard or pay the association dues."

"What'd the association do?" Kevin asked.

"Started fining him. Two hundred dollars a day. Plus legal fees."

Two hundred dollars a day? My mouth dropped open.

"The association gave them two months to fix the yard and pay the back dues."

I couldn't believe the power a homeowners' association, essentially a group of neighbors, had. "Or?"

"A lien would be taken on the house. It would be foreclosed upon after that and sold at auction to pay off debts."

No wonder Russ was under some stress. I'd be stressed out too.

Kevin shifted from foot to foot. "Where's all this stand now?"

"Well," Meredith said, "the lawsuits have been filed. The lien was placed on the house July first. It's foreclosed upon the thirty-first unless the yard is done and the fees are paid."

Unbelievable. "So Greta could lose the house?"

Meredith nodded.

"How much?" Kevin asked. "What are the fees totaling now?"

"With the legal fees? About thirty grand. That's including the daily fees of the yard not being done for the rest of this month."

Kevin whistled.

My cell phone vibrated on my hip. I looked at the readout and recognized the number immediately since I'd been calling it every hour on the hour since five o'clock yesterday.

"Tam?" I said, answering it. I backed away from Kevin and Meredith.

"I heard you killed somebody! Is it true?"

I gasped. "I didn't kill him!"

"But someone is dead?"

"Well, yeah."

"And you were involved?"

"Not technically. He had a heart attack."

"What? Hold on, Nina." She covered the phone with her hand and murmured something to someone. "Oh, all right," I heard her say. "Nina?"

"Yeah?"

"Someone wants to talk to you."

"Me?"

"Nina Ceceri?"

I sucked in a breath. "Mrs. Krauss? What are you doing there?"

"Keeping Miss Tamara company. Since you're too busy."

I think my stress level had maxed out since her jibe didn't even bother me all that much. "Did you want something?"

"Who died? Was it that awful broom lady?"

Broom lady? "Who?"

She clucked. "The trollop with my Donatelli yesterday."

Boom-Boom. Ah. "No."

"Oh." She sounded sad about it.

I couldn't help but smile. It was wrong, I know. But seeing Mrs. Krauss miserable and jealous did my heart good.

Next thing I knew Tam was back on the line, her voice muffled as she murmured something again, presumably to Mrs. Krauss.

"What was that?" I asked.

"I asked Ursula to turn the TV down." Her voice dropped to a whisper. "She snores too."

I rubbed my temple with my free hand. "How do you know that?"

"We're sharing a room."

"What!"

"She's really kind of nice."

Nice? "What kind of drugs are they giving you?"

She laughed.

"Really," I said. "How on earth did she end up in the maternity ward? Isn't she contagious?"

"Actually, I'm in the main ward. The beds were full in maternity. And the doctors said she wasn't contagious. I wouldn't risk the baby's life like that. Oh! Ana just walked in!"

"Don't tell her about the body! Don't tell—"

I heard her say, "We've got Nina on the phone! She killed some guy!"

I hung up, turned the ringer off before I got the Grand Inquisition from my cousin.

Slowly, I walked back to Kevin, whose eyes had a glazed appearance. After two seconds I knew why.

"And the Sheefers? Well, they had a Fourth of July block party one year and Russ called the police every time a firecracker went off. And the Marabellis? Well, every time they leave their kids alone, he calls Children and Family Services."

"How old are the kids?" he asked.

"Fourteen and sixteen."

Kevin sighed, held up a hand. "Thanks for your help, Mrs. Adams."

"It's Miss," she said, batting short eyelashes.

Jeez. Eww.

"Good to know," Kevin said, leading me down toward where the body had laid.

I got the shivvies again as I looked at the spot. Russ Grabinsky's body shape was still indented in the dirt.

"How'd you end up here?" Kevin asked.

"I was hired to redo this backyard. I was misled into believing it was the backyard of my client."

"Why would they mislead you?"

"Beats me."

"So you didn't have permission to work here?"

"Um, that would be no. Now Mrs. Grabinsky is threatening to sue me."

"Ouch."

"Tell me about it. She actually has a case."

"Who hired you?" he asked. "I need to talk to them."

I motioned with my head toward Lindsey Lockhart, who was standing on her driveway, her husband Bill's arms around her.

Bill, who must have known about the makeover all along.

I'd been played. I just didn't know why.

Kevin's eyes rounded. "You're kidding."

"Nope. It was your former in-laws who caused this mess."

Seven

I finally headed back to the office around six. It had been a long afternoon, and as I pulled into the TBS lot I figured by the looks of things it was about to get longer.

There were six cars in the lot, five I didn't recognize and one I did. Ana's SUV.

Let the inquisition begin.

After I parked in an open spot near the garage, I sat there thinking about how a teary Lindsey had apologized over and over for her deception.

I hadn't decided whether or not to accept the apology yet.

I leaned toward *or not.*

The air conditioner blew cold air in my face and "Rockin' Robin" played on the Oldies station as I sat in my truck trying to sort the story out.

Russ Grabinsky had a passion for healthy eating. He had the desire but not the know-how to open his own restaurant. That's where Bill had come in. Bill managed restaurants for a living and jumped at the chance to co-own one with Russ.

The two next door neighbors had banded together to create Growl. Healthy fast dining, affordable prices.

Bill and Russ had become business partners, whereas Greta

and Lindsey had become friends. According to the Lockharts, Lindsey and Bill felt just horrible over what was happening with the homeowners' association, especially since Russ hadn't put much credence into the HOA's power. Finally Bill and Lindsey decided they'd needed to step in and do something drastic to help Greta, before she lost her home. And apparently they'd had to do it on the sly because they knew that Russ was too prideful to accept help from anyone, and Greta was too reticent to go against Russ.

So they contacted me. And lied. Outright duped me, figuring no trouble would come of it because they "just knew" Greta and Russ would love the makeover once they saw it done.

Only Russ came down with the flu that was going around and went home early. And died.

And Greta, grief-stricken, lashed out.

The logistics of it all amazed me. Like how had they gotten Russ and Greta out of the house for the whole day? Turns out Russ and Greta went to the gym together every Thursday morning, and Russ went straight to work afterward. Greta, after swimming her laps, usually went home, but today had made plans to meet with Lindsey Lockhart to do a little shopping, go to lunch. Apparently a rare treat.

They'd been together when I called Lindsey, left the message about the dead guy in her yard.

Sitting in the truck, I ran my thumb over the pewter watering can key chain Riley had given me for my last birthday.

There was hope for me. Hope that once Greta had a chance to think things through, she would change her mind. Would let me finish the yard.

Wouldn't sue.

I pushed open the TBS door, and the set of chimes announced my presence.

Ana jumped up, out of Tam's throne chair.

The chimes continued to jangle, snapping my last nerve. I yanked the set off the door and flung them outside into the row of boxwoods lining the path.

Ana's eyes went wide. "Bad day?"

"No, no. Not at all." My gaze swept over the reception area. Five people I didn't know looked back at me, all wearing the same expression. Wide eyes and open mouths.

Probably I didn't make a good first impression, what with chucking the chimes out the door and all.

Sue me.

Sue me. I laughed, cracking myself up.

"Um, Nina. I set up some interviews with some prospects for Tam's job. To fill in, while she's gone."

I checked them out. All still wore that *Warning! Warning! In the same room as a crazy lady* look.

Two men, three women. All looked respectable, and I had trouble figuring out what they'd done that landed them in Ana's world. I'd never gotten a single guess right, so I didn't try too hard.

All in all, Ana's probationers had worked out for me. I'd gotten burned only a few times. Like the time Pedro Cho drove away on one of my John Deeres, never to return. Or the time Ike Hughes took a deposit for a job and disappeared. The authorities tracked him to a Disney Magic cruise ship, where he'd been whooping it up with Mickey on my dime.

I thought again about not hiring any more probationers. "Ana, I don't think—"

"What's a few interviews?" she asked, hands on hips.

All I wanted to do was wrap up a few loose ends, go home, shower, and crawl into bed for the next three days.

Then I spotted a box of Almond Joys on Tam's desk, with a bow on them.

Bobby. He sent me Almond Joys on a regular basis.

I sighed. What was I going to do about him? The last time he'd dropped me off at home after dinner, he looked at me with those big blue eyes and asked, "Can I come in?"

I'd lied and told him Riley was home.

Ack.

I'm sure he knew I lied, but he didn't call me on it. He just kissed me till I couldn't breathe and walked away.

"Nina?" Ana asked.

Thinking of Bobby lightened my mood. It always did. "All right," I reluctantly agreed. "Send someone into my office."

"Mary Hernandez?" Ana said. "You're first."

A petite woman with long dark hair and darkly tanned skin stood up, walked hesitantly toward the office. "I'll be right in," I said and offered her a drink. She shook her head no.

"So," Ana said as I walked toward the fridge for a Dr Pepper fix, "the dead guy . . . did you really kill him?"

Heads snapped up, stared at me. "I didn't kill anyone!" I cried. "He just happened to . . . well, die while I was there."

Mary hustled out of my office, saying something to Ana in Spanish. She hurried out the door and was followed by three others.

One man stayed, a *Better Homes and Gardens* magazine forgotten on his lap as he stared at me.

"Really, I didn't kill him," I said to him. "He had a heart attack."

"Did he turn blue?" Ana asked.

Ana had a sick fascination with dead people. She wanted to know all the details.

"Ana," I warned.

"Purple? Did he get all stiff?"

I thought about Russ lying there, a prostrate stick figure, and shuddered.

"Foaming at the mouth?"

"I am not having this conversation."

"You," I said to the man on the couch. "What's your name?"

"Harry von Barber."

"Nina, I'm going to head out now." I jumped as someone came out of the conference room to my left.

"Jeez! A little warning. A slight cough or something! I didn't even know you were here."

Jean-Claude apologized, then said, "I was hiding out after . . . well, you know."

Yeah, I did know. But maybe Kit wouldn't kill him after what happened with the dead guy and all.

He went on. "I've been working on the next job, doing some ordering."

"Good," I said, thinking maybe I wouldn't have to fire him after all.

"Jean-Claude?" Harry asked. "Is that you, man?"

My head snapped to Harry, then to Ana, who shrugged.

Jean-Claude's cheeks turned a fiery red. "Do I know you?"

I caught a very subtle shake of Jean-Claude's head as he asked. Hmmm.

Harry cleared his throat. "Guess not. You just look familiar."

My mouth dropped open. "You knew his name!"

"Lots of people with that name." Harry shrugged, fussed with his collar.

"Uh-huh. Jean-Claude is at the top of every baby name list. I'll have to let Tam know."

"Tam?" Harry asked.

"I better go." Jean-Claude fairly sprinted out the door.

Obviously Harry knew Jean-Claude and Jean-Claude didn't want anyone to know that. Why? Did it have something to do with the late night activities he was so hush-hush about?

Had Harry been into the car stealing business too? Maybe

a drug dealer? Maybe he'd been arrested on possession charges. Asking him might shed some light on Jean-Claude's nighttime forays.

"Hey, Harry, why were you arrested?" I asked.

He looked at Ana, his eyes pained. "Do I have to tell her that?"

Ana nodded. " 'Fraid so."

"I, um. Shhrohghn," he said, rubbing his hand over his mouth.

"What?"

He pulled his hand away. "Solicitation, all right?"

I blinked. "You're a prostitute?"

"I prefer escort. And I'll have you know I was entrapped. That's why I got locked up."

Harry was, er, an escort. And he knew Jean-Claude.

Oh. My. God. Was Jean-Claude moonlighting as a gigolo?

"I have to go talk to her, right?" I asked. "Try to explain."

It was early Saturday morning and I should have been helping Kit with a "mini"—a mini makeover reserved for smaller yards or certain problem areas—but I knew the McPhains' yard was perfectly fine in his capable hands. Plus, he had Marty and Jean-Claude with him. Despite my determination to fire Jean-Claude, I'd taken pity on him since he had been at the Grabinsky site after all—helping Kit.

I was such a sucker. How many chances was I going to give him?

Kit had plenty of manpower to transform a small nondescript brick patio into something special. Plus, if he needed help he could always call Deanna or Coby, who were at the office.

Instead of helping out, I'd driven over to see Tam.

"I don't know," Tam said. "It might make things worse."

"Worse than getting sued?" I asked.

The tortuous beltlike contraption around her waist was still there. And it had a friend. I could see two squarish lumps underneath her hot pink silk pajama shirt. She'd explained to me that one monitored contractions, the other the baby's heart rate. As of right now, everything was normal. The medication she was taking had stopped the contractions. But she wasn't going anywhere anytime soon.

Which meant I had to find a temp for her.

But not Harry.

I didn't dare tell her about Jean-Claude possibly being a gigolo. That might send her into irreversible labor.

A notepad balanced on Tam's belly. She tapped a pencil on it. "You have a point."

"For once," Brickhouse Krauss piped in.

"Don't you have some oxygen to suck?" I asked in a too sweet voice.

"Oh!" Tam said, clutching her stomach.

"What? Is it the baby?" I glanced at the monitors, but everything looked okay. "Should I get the doctor?"

"No, no," Tam assured me.

Brickhouse had looked ready to leap out of the bed to be of assistance. Actually, she looked rather healthy to me. Pink cheeks, softly glowing skin. What was she still doing here?

"The baby just kicked a rib is all."

I glanced at her stomach in time to see a bump move from one side of her body to the other.

Tam laughed.

"What?" I asked.

"You should see your face."

"Does it always do that?" I asked, horrified. It was like something out of a horror movie.

Tam nodded. "You get used to it."

"Oh." I didn't believe her for a minute. You get used to swimming in lukewarm water. You get used to doing your hair the same way. You get used to infomercials. You do not get used to someone poking you from the inside out.

"How about the name Jake?" Tam asked, picking up the notepad, pencil poised.

Mrs. Krauss clucked. "Jake Munroe used to pick his nose in my class."

Tam crossed that name off her list. "Jane?"

I made a face. "Jane Albertson stole my boyfriend in the first grade."

Tam and Mrs. Krauss stared at me.

"What?" I asked. "I'm not allowed to hold a grudge?"

Tam crossed that name off her list. "Kevin?"

I gave her the Ceceri Evil Eye.

"All right." She scratched off that name too.

I got to thinking again about Greta Grabinsky. Maybe going to see her, pleading my case, wasn't the wisest move. Maybe I should give her time. A few days at least. But if she sued . . .

I'd worked too hard to lose it all.

"What could she do, really?" I asked.

"Are we back to that?" Mrs. Krauss asked, flipping through a baby name book.

"Well, I'm sorry to bore you, but I don't know what to do."

"The worst she could do is throw you out," Tam said. "Michael?"

"Michael Perry cheated on his tenth grade term paper," Mrs. Krauss said in a way that made me think he'd paid dearly for it. "Bought one from an upperclassman."

I thought that was pretty ingenious of him. I'd slaved over mine, "A Socioeconomic Analysis of *Romeo and Juliet,*" and had gotten a D.

Considering I now couldn't tell you what *socioeconomic* meant probably meant I earned that D.

Brickhouse narrowed her ice blue eyes at Tam. "I know you don't want your son to have a cheater's name."

Tam scratched that one off the list too.

To me, Mrs. Krauss said, "She could call the cops on you. Harassment." She clucked, then smiled as if the idea amused her.

The last thing I wanted was to be involved with the police. Especially one homicide detective in particular. I wondered when Russ Grabinsky's autopsy would be completed. Freedom, Ohio, wasn't exactly the murder capital of the country. How busy could the M.E. be?

"Patrika?" Mrs. Krauss offered.

Tam and I frowned at her.

She clucked and continued to flip pages.

"I wouldn't do it," Tam said. "Going to see the dead man's wife is asking for trouble, Nina."

"Ach. I agree," Brickhouse added.

That pretty much sealed it for me. I had to go see Mrs. Grabinsky. Get her to listen to me. If only to prove to Mrs. Krauss that she was wrong.

"How did it go with Jean-Claude?" Tam asked.

"Well, um . . ."

"You didn't fire him!"

"I couldn't."

Mrs. Krauss clucked. "You're a wuss, Nina Ceceri."

I bit my tongue to keep from calling Mrs. Krauss something I might regret later. Actually, I wouldn't regret it at all. "Oh yeah? Well, you're—"

"Looking good," Mr. Cabrera said to Brickhouse from the doorway. He held a pot of red geraniums.

"Donatelli!" Mrs. Krauss's whole face brightened. She clucked lovingly. "Geraniums. My favorites."

Geraniums always reminded me of cemeteries, but I kept that tidbit to myself. No need to remind Mrs. Krauss of Mr. Cabrera's bad luck with women.

Mrs. Krauss abandoned the baby name book and leaned up for a kiss.

It lasted for a good ten seconds.

Eww.

"I've got to go." Quickly, I kissed Tam's cheek good-bye, rubbed her belly, hoped the baby wouldn't move while I did it and creep me out. It didn't. "I'll come back later," I said.

"Leaving so soon, Miz Quinn?" Mr. Cabrera asked.

"Sorry," I said, not sorry at all. "I've got someone to see."

Tam's and Brickhouse's groans followed me out the door.

Eight

I parked down the block. I told myself it was because I needed the exercise—my lungs still hadn't recovered from that sprint after BeBe—but really, it was because I didn't want to give Mrs. Grabinsky any advanced warning. If she saw me coming, she might not open the door. We weren't exactly on friendly terms.

Skipping over a crack in the sidewalk, I glanced at the Lockharts' house. A stone path flanked by blooming flower beds led to the front door. It was a charming house. Cape Cod style with dormers and a front porch complete with two rocking chairs and hanging flower baskets—petunias with flowing ivy.

The lawn sported a few clumps of crabgrass, which made me feel better. Lindsey wasn't a complete perfectionist.

I glanced toward the big picture window. It would be so easy to peek in.

Maybe see if there were any frames set out.

That might hold pictures of loved ones.

Dead loved ones.

I glanced up, then down the street. No sign of any HOA patrols.

The Lockharts had a side garage, and I decided to check

and see if it was open before I played Peeping Tom. Trying not to look suspicious, I moseyed down the sidewalk. The two-car garage door was open wide, a Jetta parked on one side, the other side empty.

From her visits to my office, I knew Lindsey drove a newer model Escalade. So Bill was home. Odd. I'd have thought he'd be busy at work today, especially since he was now running Growl alone.

I abandoned my peeping ideas—for now—and turned my attention to the Grabinskys' yard.

It was a mess. Yellow crime scene tape still cordoned off the backyard, and I wondered why. The forensic guys should have been here and gone by now. Not that there was anything to find. Russ had had a heart attack, plain and simple.

Nothing's ever plain and simple, my inner voice warned.

I didn't want to listen to it, but couldn't help but hear the ring of truth.

By the looks of things, Russ Grabinsky hadn't been Man of the Year. But murder? Who'd want to kill him?

And how? Poisoning? An overdose?

Shaking my head, I decided not to go there. It had been a heart attack. I needed to stop playing Quincy, M.E., and get on with why I was here.

I needed to conjure up my inner Pollyanna and convince one seriously ticked-off woman not to sue me.

Since the yard was a mess anyway, I abandoned my manners and cut across the lawn. Three small concrete steps with a rusting black iron railing led to the front door.

The pansies on the front step looked in need of some water. I looked for the spigot, but raised voices coming from inside distracted me.

A man and a woman were arguing, but I couldn't make out what they were saying.

As usual, my nosiness got the better of me. I leaned over the step's railing and peered into the front window. The front room looked to be a small family room, straight from the fifties. There was an old-fashioned TV and radio. A rotary phone and a powder blue Smith-Corona typewriter sat on a rolltop desk in the corner. Bookshelves were stuffed full, but orderly. There were no pictures, I noticed. Not even an obligatory wedding one. A faded pink love seat with a tattered throw blanket balled into one of its corners sat diagonally from two worn La-Z-Boys. A *TV Guide* rested on the ottoman in front of a leather chair in front of the window. On a table next to the chair, I saw a stack of bound books. Old-fashioned accounting books, by the looks of the spiral bounds and red leather. I'd used them before Tam brought me into the computer age.

Beyond an arched doorway, I could see shadows coming from what appeared to be the kitchen area (the refrigerator was a dead giveaway), but still couldn't see who was arguing.

The woman had to be Greta Grabinsky. But who was the man? Did this have anything to do with Russ's death?

Had it been murder after all? A love triangle gone wrong?

I shuddered at the thought of Greta Grabinsky being in the middle of a love triangle.

Love is blind, my inner voice reminded.

Oh great. Now *it* was sounding like my mother too.

I turned toward the street, looked left, then right.

Trying to look natural, I eased off the step, made a beeline for the backyard. Ducking under the crime scene tape, I looked over my shoulder to make sure no one was watching, then hurried around the corner, bumping into something hard. Someone, actually. A man.

He spun around, annoyed eyes widening when he saw me.

Half scared to death, I opened my mouth to scream, but only a gurgle came out.

"Shh!" Bill Lockhart warned, holding a finger up to his lips. He pressed on the top of my head, ducking me down even though I was a good two inches shorter than the height of the windowsill. He turned his back to me, his ear cocked.

My heart raced, but I managed to close my mouth. Blood pulsed through my ears, drowning out the voices inside the house. Adrenaline surged through my body, looking for an outlet. I swear I could see my chest pulsating beneath my T-shirt, my heart still pounding.

Was this what it was like to have a heart attack? The chest pain, the lack of air?

I couldn't help but look at the spot where Russ had fallen. To me, it looked like he had died quickly. I wondered if he'd actually suffered silently, a scream trapped in his throat.

Oh great. Now I was thinking like Ana.

I drew in a deep breath, let it out. I did that a few more times, glad I had seen Tam practicing her Lamaze breathing.

When I finally felt my pulse slowing, I whispered, "What are you doing here?"

He looked over his shoulder. "Same as you, I suspect. Shh."

Trying to talk Greta out of suing. I'd forgotten she threatened Lindsey with a lawsuit too.

Now that I had calmed a bit, I could hear the voices inside, through the open window above our heads.

"Greta," the man said, "don't play games with me. You'll be the one who gets hurt by them."

"Is that a threat?" I heard her say.

"Who's she talking to?" I whispered.

Bill shrugged.

"No, it's a promise," the man inside said.

I groaned.

I noticed Bill had ear hair as he said, "What?"

"What a lame line! 'No, it's a promise,' " I mocked. "Gag me. Obviously it's someone who watches too many B movies."

"You talk a lot."

"It's the adrenaline."

"I know Russ had them," the male voice said. "If he had them, you had them. And I want them back. Now. Russ had no right to them and neither do you."

The man's voice was young. Maybe twenties or thirties. This put my love triangle theory into serious doubt.

"What do you think he had?" I asked.

"If you'd be quiet maybe we'd find out."

Greta's voice was hard but tired. She sounded stressed. "I told you, I don't have whatever you're looking for. I don't know anything about it."

I eyed the kitchen window. Even if I stood up straight I wouldn't be able to see in. I looked at Bill. He seemed like a strong guy. "Boost me up."

Bill looked over his shoulder at me. "What?"

"Boost me up." I motioned toward the window. "I want to see who she's talking to."

The male's voice lacked patience. "The only reason the lawsuit is being dropped is so I could get them back."

Lawsuit dropped? The HOA lawsuit? "Did you know about that?" I asked Bill. According to Lindsey and Bill, the reason they paid for the Grabinskys' surprise makeover—and lied to me—was to prevent the older couple from being foreclosed upon by the HOA. But if the lawsuit had been dropped, then why go through all the trouble?

Bill made a makeshift sling with his hands. "No."

What would the Lockharts have gained by paying for the backyard makeover if there wasn't a lawsuit? People didn't spend twenty thousand dollars out of neighborly love, even if they had to look at a hideous backyard.

The male voice inside the house carried easily through the open window. "I don't like being blackmailed, Greta."

Someone had been blackmailed to have the lawsuit dropped. Blackmailed by Russ, apparently.

Definitely a motive for murder.

Not that Russ was murdered.

It had been a heart attack.

If I kept thinking that, then maybe it'd be true.

I slipped my foot into Bill's linked hands and used the brick exterior for leverage.

I stayed to the left of the window and peered in, a quick peep just to see where the two were standing. Greta stood in front of the sink, her back to me. All I could see of the man was his hands as he gestured. He stood too far left, near the back door.

"I want them back, Greta."

He wore a wedding ring. Not just a simple band. There was something unusual about it, but I was too far away to make out any details. I looked for a watch or any other identifying feature, but couldn't find anything that stood out. Only man hands. Long fingers, short nails—not bitten. He must have worn a short-sleeve shirt because I couldn't see any cuffs.

"Who is it?" Bill asked.

"I can't see him," I whispered.

The back door creaked open. "I want them back by—"

I didn't hear the rest. I fell backward when Bill released his hands. I braced for a crash landing but was snatched up before I hit the ground.

Bill pushed me around the corner of the house just as the back door slammed closed.

I dragged Bill toward the front of the house, but he resisted.

Breathing hard, I tried to keep my voice low. "What're you doing?"

"Going back. I want to see who it is. I'll look casual."

He was nuts. I was so out of there.

As he stuck his hands in his pockets, started whistling "Yellow Rose of Texas," and headed for the police tape, I made a break for the front yard . . . and almost slammed into someone when I rounded the corner.

What was it with me crashing into people today?

"Who are you?" Suspicious eyes honed in. "What are you doing sneaking around? I'm going to call the police!" she said, shaking a finger at me.

Backing up, I scrambled for an answer. She was a short rotund woman, with thick arms and thicker ankles. She wore orthopedic shoes, black stirrup pants from the eighties, a purple beaded shirt, and a strange glint in her eye.

I quickly said, "I'm Nina Quinn. I'm the landscaper . . . I was just checking to see if the crime scene tape had been removed yet. I'd like to finish the job I started."

I was such a good liar. I wasn't sure if this was a good trait or not. Probably not, but a girl had to make do with the gifts given her.

Bill came whistling around the corner and stiffened when he saw the woman. "Noreen?" he said. "What are you doing here? Aren't you supposed to be at wo—"

She cut him off. "Are you two together?" Her gaze jumped between Bill and me, suspicion still apparent. Potato-shaped, she looked to be about fifty, with a short graying bob with chunky bangs, chubby cheeks, and big Sally Jesse Raphael red glasses.

"Us?" I said. "No. Definitely not."

We all jumped when the front door swung open, banging against the wall behind it. Seemed I wasn't the only one on edge.

A red-faced, perspiring Greta filled the doorway.

"Greta, what's wrong?" Mrs. Potato Head asked.

Greta still wore the same housecoat as yesterday. "What are you all doing here?"

I swallowed hard. It was quite clear by her jumpy demeanor and angry eyes that she wasn't in the mood for visitors. This probably wasn't the best time to ask about dropping the lawsuit. "I, um, came by to talk."

Bill said, "Me too."

Mrs. Potato Head didn't say anything, but Greta didn't seem to be looking for an answer from her. Greta folded meaty arms across her huge chest. "I have nothing to say to either of you."

Ohh-kay.

I looked to Bill. He took a step forward, toward the front stairs. "Greta, I'm truly sorry about Russ, you must know that."

Her shoulders stiffened. "I don't know anything right now."

"Fair enough," he said. "But—"

Greta glared. Her beehive 'do shook as she leaned against the doorjamb. "But what? What do you want, Bill?"

I saw his pointy Adam's apple bob as he said, "Russ had taken some paperwork home with him from the restaurant. I need it."

"It'll have to wait."

"It really can't."

"It has to." She wiped her forehead with the top of her hand. "Go home."

Bill held out his hands, pleading. "Greta, please."

I didn't understand the hint of desperation I heard in Bill's voice. Was he looking for the account books I'd seen through the window? Were they for Growl? Or was he looking for something else? Something so important that he'd leave his pride behind and beg a grieving widow?

"No." Greta's jaw set stubbornly. "I don't wish to see anyone right now. Go away."

She looked at wit's end. Russ's death had obviously taken its toll. Not to mention the conversation from the mystery man in her kitchen.

Mrs. Potato Head climbed the front steps, paused on the landing, adjusted her glasses, and glowered at us as well. Hmmph. Nothing like feeling welcome.

"You heard her," Mrs. Potato Head said. "The both of you need to leave. Greta needs to rest."

"You too, Noreen," Greta said. "I want to be alone."

A look of hurt flashed across Mrs. Potato Head's face. "I can understand that, but now is the time you should be with family."

Although Bill and I had been dismissed, neither of us made ready to leave. Apparently I wasn't the only one with a nosy streak.

Or was he waiting until everyone left to talk his way into the Grabinsky house?

Greta reached out, touched Noreen's arm. Her voice had softened noticeably. "Thanks, but no. I truly wish to be alone."

When Greta turned to go back into the house, I noted that she and Noreen had the same profile . . . and without the Sally Jesse glasses, the same eyes. Sisters, probably.

Greta closed the door with much more caution than when she'd opened it.

Well. I couldn't say this was a wasted trip, not with overhearing Greta being threatened.

Russ had been a blackmailer. Wasn't that interesting?

And Bill was desperate to find "paperwork."

Noreen came down the steps, her chin held high. False bravado, if the tears in her eyes were any indication.

"Noreen, may I have a word with you?" A strained smile tugged at Bill's lips.

She sniffed, and looked directly at Bill without blinking.

"Now's not a good time. I'm worried about my sister. Greta isn't used to being alone."

Aha! They were sisters. Good to know my Clue-playing skills could actually come in handy once in a while.

Bill spoke through clenched teeth. "When, then?"

Noreen wrung her hands. "I'll be around."

I looked between the two of them. "You two know each other well?"

Without answering, Noreen said, "I must go." She hurried down the front walk, opened the door to a small compact, and drove away.

I looked a question at Bill.

"Not very well," he said.

My eyebrow arched.

"Did you see the man from the kitchen?"

"He was gone by the time I made it back there. I've got to go too."

My other eyebrow arched as he walked away, but I wasn't sure why. All I knew was that my instincts were rarely wrong. Bill and Lindsey's explanation about hiring me just wasn't ringing true.

I walked back to my truck with a lot of questions.

Who was blackmailing Greta?

Who had Russ been blackmailing?

And the most important . . .

Had Russ been murdered?

Nine

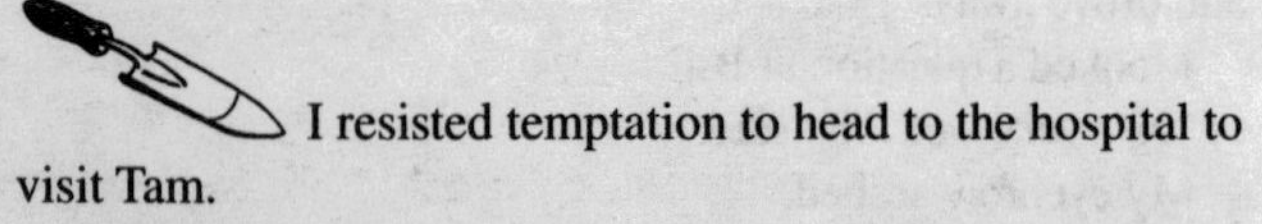

I resisted temptation to head to the hospital to visit Tam.

Okay, okay, so I didn't want to hear Brickhouse's "I told you so" about my disastrous visit with Greta.

It was closing in on two o' clock, and as I headed to the office to get some paperwork done, I called Kit to make sure the mini was going okay.

He answered his cell on the third ring. "Yo."

"What kind of greeting is that?"

"My kind."

I imagined him winking when he said it. He had a playful tone in his voice. "Everything going okay?"

"No dead bodies."

"Ha. Ha."

"The brick pavers are laid, the fire pit is done, the flowers are going in now. We should be back at the office in another two hours or so."

"Did Jean-Claude show up?"

"Ten minutes late. Looks like death warmed up and spit out."

I didn't want to think about death. I turned right onto Jay-bird, heading toward TBS.

"He say anything?" I ventured. "About what he's been doing?" I'd kept my gigolo suspicions to myself. Well, I'd shared them with Ana, who said she'd look into it.

I wondered exactly what kind of connections she had in that area, but truly, there were some things about my cousin even I didn't want to know.

"Nah."

"Any suspicions?"

"Nah."

I rolled my eyes. "You're so helpful."

"That's what you pay me for," he said, and I heard a big *WOOF* in the background.

"Is that BeBe?"

"I, um—" Static suddenly filled the line "You're breaking up!"

"Kit," I warned, knowing exactly what he was doing. Another *WOOF* echoed across the line.

"Gotta go, Nina."

I stared at my silent cell phone. He'd hung up on me.

Hmmph.

Part of me wanted to go to the site and find out why BeBe was once again part of my crew. BeBe was sweet and all, but a work site was no place for her. She could possibly cause more damage than we could fix.

If BeBe couldn't stay at home, then it was time for doggy day care.

I walked into the office and found I kind of missed the chimes.

Coby manned Tam's desk. He looked up at me, the phone balanced between his ear and shoulder, one hand on the computer keyboard, the other holding a pencil.

"Do you know how to schedule an appointment?" he asked me. Then said into the phone, "No, no, not you."

He mouthed *Help me* and added big puppy dog eyes.

His chubby baby-fat cheeks were covered in a light peach fuzzy blond that would someday turn to stubble.

I had to imagine that, at twenty-four, he hoped "one day" would be soon.

I took the phone, sorted out the mess, and hung up.

"We need to get a temp," Coby said, rising from Tam's throne. It had been odd to see him sitting there, and not Tam. She was such a fixture in the office. Her African violet, Sassy, even seemed to droop a little. I made a mental note to take it to the hospital with me the next time I visited.

"Thanks for covering things today," I said.

He took a set of keys from his pocket, headed toward the door. "I've got a cousin who needs a job."

"Any experience?"

He hedged. "Define experience."

"As in telephone, computer, people skills?"

"Ah, no."

"Then I'm going to have to pass."

"You're missing out," he said, shaking a finger.

"I'll risk it."

He waved as he walked out. I wondered if anyone else was there. I checked around but didn't see anyone, and wondered where Deanna was until I played my voice mail and discovered that she'd called in sick today because her two-year-old son Lucah had that weird flu going around.

I wondered what it was like to have a two-year-old. I didn't have much experience with babies or toddlers. I'd met Riley when he was eight. Though I supposed if I could survive his attitude, then I could face anything.

This summer flu going around had hit hard. I wondered if that's what Russ had had. Could that have played a factor in his death?

Tossing aside thoughts of death, I wandered into Deanna's office and couldn't help but peek at her design plan for a mini scheduled for the following afternoon.

Since she'd shown so much design promise, I'd given her free reign over the project. She'd been ear-splittingly happy. I knew Kit was scheduled to be her project foreman and realized he'd been working a lot lately. Not that he complained—he rarely expressed his unhappiness. Maybe it was time to hire another contractor to lessen Kit's load?

Or maybe it was time to cut back altogether. I'd been thinking about it more and more lately. The long hours were wearing thin on all of us.

Looking around, I realized I missed the darn chimes. I went outside to look and found them in a boxwood near my TBS truck. As I reattached them to the door, the phone rang.

I gave Sassy a pat as I picked up the phone on Tam's desk. "Taken by Surprise, this is Nina Quinn."

"This is your date, wondering where you are."

My date. Oh no! "I'm so sorry, Bobby! I forgot." We'd had plans to go to a Reds game. "It's been crazy here." I'd talked to him last night, told him all about what had happened. "The widow is still threatening to sue me. I hate to say it, but she has a case."

"My cousin Josh is a lawyer. A good one. Let me call him for you."

I had independence issues and thought I should call my own lawyer, but decided I needed help. I couldn't do it all, as much as I wanted to. "All right."

"How about dinner and a movie now that the game is just about over?" he asked.

"Bobby, I'm so sorry I forgot about the game!"

"It's okay. They're losing anyway. Dinner? Movie? It will take your mind off things for a while."

I agreed before I thought too much about it, and hung up before I changed my mind.

I knew I needed to decide how I felt about Bobby. Soon. I didn't want to hurt him.

The phone rang again, reminding me that I also needed to find a temp for Tam, though no one could ever replace her. She was the backbone of TBS. She kept things running smoothly, me organized, and track of all loose ends.

Not to mention she answered the phone.

"Taken by Surprise, this is Nina Quinn."

"You're too busy to be answering the phone."

Tam. I smiled.

"You really need to find a fill-in for me."

"I know."

"Let me call a few people. I'll have them there Monday at ten A.M."

"Okay."

"Wait. Check the schedule. Make sure you don't have anything going on."

I checked the schedule, feeling a little bit like a kid being told what to do.

"Nothing," I said.

"I'll take care of it."

"You really should be resting."

"All I do is rest."

She had a point.

"How'd the visit to the dead guy's wife go?"

I hedged.

"I told you so," she said.

I heard corroborating clucking in the background and groaned. "I gotta go," I said.

"Liar."

"'Bye!"

I hung up, switched on the voice-mail system, and tried to get some work done.

Ten

"Do you want to have kids?"

I choked on my coconut ice cream, spitting some out, which was a shame because it was *really* good.

Bobby patted my back, a smile pulling at the corners of his lips.

"Sorry," he said. "Just trying to get your attention."

We were at StarBright, an old-fashioned drive-in movie theater. A speaker box was hooked over Bobby's half-lowered window as *Star Wars*—the original—played on the big screen.

"Well, you've got it now." I wiped a speck of coconut from the dashboard.

I'd been a crappy date. So lost in thoughts over lawsuits and blackmailers I hadn't paid Bobby any attention at all. I was wasting prime drive-in make-out time.

"You thinking about that dead guy?"

Sadly, I stared at what was left of my little cup of ice cream. I'd lost my appetite. "Yeah."

"Everything will work out."

"Wish I could believe that."

I must have sounded pathetic because he rubbed a knuckle over my cheek, leaned in and kissed me. I tried to move closer to him, but he drove a Celica that had bucket seats and one of the boxes in the middle that was a car's equivalent of a kitchen junk drawer. Whatever happened to good old-fashioned bench seats? Did some sort of abstinence group have them outlawed?

A car honked next to us, followed by a series of "Woo-hoo, Mr. MacKenna."

I'm sure I was blushing, but glad it was dark so the teens in the car next to us couldn't see.

Bobby wiped his lips, gave a little wave to the group. "Students," he said.

"I figured."

"Maybe we should go somewhere private?" he asked, a husky tone to his voice.

Panic swelled. This. Was. It.

Could I really do it?

It wasn't as though I didn't like Bobby. I really did. And it wasn't as though my body wasn't begging for me to say okay. It was.

I just . . .

"You're thinking too much," Bobby said, leaning in to kiss me again.

More honking ensued from the car next to us, but I couldn't have cared less. Bobby either, apparently, because he didn't pull back right away.

When he finally did, he looked at me, saying nothing.

I tried to catch my breath, and finally said, "Private is good."

He fairly chucked the speaker box out the window, started the car, throwing it into reverse. The kids next to us cheered.

"Riley's not home, right?"

My libido was doing a happy dance. "He's not home." He spent most weekends with Kevin.

Kevin.

No, no, no! Don't think about him, I told myself.

Over and over again.

Because apparently it was the only thing I *could* think about right now. I needed distraction. Immediately.

I reached over, took Bobby's hand as he sped through the streets. "So," I said, picking up his line of questioning, "do you want kids?"

He didn't hesitate. "Yes."

"How many?"

"At least four."

"Four!" All right. This might not have been the best distraction.

He laughed. "You should see your face."

I could imagine.

"I want a big family." He rubbed a finger along the palm of my hand, sending delicious shivers up my arm.

"Oh."

"You never did answer me, by the way."

"What? When?"

"Do *you* want kids?"

This was probably one of those conversations all people should have at some point in their relationship, but now, on the way to do what we were going to do, I didn't think it was the best time.

"Nina?" He sounded worried. "You don't want kids at all?"

"No, I do. I do. I don't know about four, but I do want kids. Someday."

He glanced at me. "Someday?"

"Someday." I didn't know when. How did a person know when?

In the streetlight, I could see him nod. "I suppose we should just get it all out."

"All?"

"Everything."

"Like?" I asked, wishing my ice cream wasn't a puddle in a cup on the floorboard. I could use some fortification right now.

"How do you feel about marriage?"

I groaned.

"Well, that answers that."

"Don't get me wrong. I think I could marry again . . ."

"Someday."

"Exactly."

I noticed his finger had stopped rubbing my palm.

"What about relocating?" he asked.

"Relocating? Where?"

"Anywhere."

Moving? I just couldn't see it. This is where my family was. As dysfunctional as they were, I loved them and couldn't imagine not being near them. And work . . . Tam, Kit.

And Riley.

"I don't think so."

I wondered at the turn in the conversation. A rather large part of me wished we were back at the drive-in, making out.

Hating the silence, I struggled to find something to say to ease the sudden tension.

And couldn't find one thing.

Mostly because my thoughts kept turning back to Russ Grabinsky. I was debating whether or not I should call Kevin about the man who threatened Greta.

Then I kept thinking that I should just stay out of it.

But . . . The man from Greta's kitchen had had a very identifiable wedding ring. If I could just find him . . .

No, no, no, my inner voice chanted.

And what about Bill and Lindsey? Why had they hired me if the lawsuit against the Grabinskys had been dropped? Had they really not known? Was it even true?

Then it hit me. The lawsuit. The man in Greta's kitchen had said he'd had it dropped. All I needed to do was find out who'd been behind it. Then I'd know who threatened Greta. And who had motive to kill Russ.

If Russ had been murdered.

That was a big if.

Though the more I learned about Russ Grabinsky, the more I wondered why he hadn't been bumped off before now.

". . . feel about being a stay-at-home mom?"

My head snapped up as I caught the tail end of what Bobby had been saying.

He laughed.

"Sorry," I said.

"The lawsuit?" he asked as he turned onto my street. "I called Josh but he hasn't gotten back to me yet."

Josh. His cousin, the lawyer. Who I prayed could get me out of this mess. "I can't help it," I said.

The Mill was relatively silent. I noticed that Mr. Cabrera's house was dark, but his big red Pontiac, aka the Beast, was parked in his driveway.

My gaze automatically skipped to Boom-Boom's house, where it was also dark. I wondered what was going on between the two of them, if anything. After all, Mr. Cabrera had been kissing Brickhouse just that morning.

However, I wouldn't put two-timing past him.

Bobby cut the engine, turned to me. "Well, I think I know how to get you to stop thinking all together."

My mouth went dry. "Yeah?"

"Oh yeah. Let's go in."

I walked up the front steps. Okay, so I ran up them. Big

deal. As I dug around in my backpack for my keys, Bobby wrapped his arms around me, kissed my neck.

Keys, keys, keys, I repeated to myself, trying to concentrate.

I tipped my head up, bit my lip when he found a sensitive spot under my ear. And froze.

"What?" Bobby asked, looking around.

"My lights are on inside."

"And?"

"I haven't been home since this morning. I didn't leave them on."

"Maybe Riley?"

"He's at Kevin's."

"Maybe he came home early?" he asked, then mumbled something about bad luck.

"Kevin would have called."

"Maybe we should call the police?"

As I debated this, my front door flung open. "*Chérie!* You're home!"

I stared in disbelief. "Mom?"

"Is she finally here?" I heard.

My eyes widened. "Maria?"

"Bobby!" My mother air-kissed his cheeks.

My sister Maria did the same.

"What are you two doing here?" I asked, still staring.

"A surprise makeover! Surprise! We parked down the block and everything!"

"Wh-What?" I mumbled.

"For your house. Really, Nina, it was so outdated," Maria said. Her long blonde hair was pulled back into a fancy chignon, and only she could look gorgeous in a pair of overalls. Paint splattered the front of them.

Orange paint.

Oh dear God. She was painting something orange.

In my house.

I had to stop her.

Just as I opened my mouth, my mother said, "Now, now, *chérie*. I know this must be overwhelming, but it must be done. No arguing."

"But—"

My mother stood firm. "No buts. Knickers and knots, Nina. Knickers and knots."

"Want to rethink relocating?" Bobby joked from behind me.

I turned and gave him the Ceceri Evil Eye. It had no effect whatsoever, which told me a lot. Men not affected by the Ceceri Evil Eye were keepers.

The forever after kind of keepers.

I swallowed hard.

"Where's Dad?" I asked.

My mother waved a manicured hand, tucked a loose piece of blonde hair behind her ear. "Off doing whatever he does on Saturday nights."

"You don't know what he does?"

She waved off my concern. "Some club or another. Historians Unite, or some such."

Ohh-kay. I looked to Maria. "Where's Nate?"

"Boys' weekend. They're fishing," she said with a grossed-out look. No wonder she hadn't been asked along. "Took the dog with him, thank God."

Gracie, a Chihuahua, was as high maintenance as my sister.

Bobby leaned down, his breath warm against my ear. Oh yeah. Now I remembered why we were in a rush to get here. "We could go to my place."

My mother's eyes lit. "His place!" She turned to Maria. "Did you hear that? His place!"

I closed my eyes, wishing I had relocated a long time ago.

"It's about time," Maria said to me. "Maybe you'll stop being so testy."

I stepped forward, fists clenched. "I'll show you testy."

Bobby grabbed my arm.

"Snappy too," Maria added.

I heard Bobby sigh. I knew the feeling. I turned to face him. "I think I maybe need to stay here tonight."

He smiled. God, I loved his smile. "It's okay."

"No, it's not!" my mother said. "Go with him. Go! Go!"

What did it say about my life that my mother was prodding me to go home with a man?

"Orange," I said to Bobby under my breath, by way of explanation.

"Come on," he said. "Walk me to my car."

He opened the Celica's door, gave me a hug, held me close.

As we stood there, a whirring noise caught my attention. I looked up just in time to see a golf cart whizzing down the street, Boom-Boom at the wheel, Mr. Cabrera next to her.

Brickhouse was going to kill him.

Boom-Boom beeped and waved at us as she swerved into her driveway.

"If you change your mind . . ." Bobby said, leaving the offer dangling.

"I'll call."

He gave me a quick kiss, ducked into the car. The engine purred to life. "Nina," he said.

"Hmm?"

"We really do need to talk," he said.

My heart backpedaled.

Talk? Talk was never good.

"Why? About what?"

His eyebrows dipped. "I've got something important to ask you."

"Me?" Oh. My. God. He had something to *ask* me?

"Yes you."

"Oh." Panic set in. My stomach churned.

"Maybe tomorrow?"

I nodded and closed the door. He waved as he backed out of the driveway. I watched him drive away, then turned toward my house.

Orange.

Ugh.

Instead of going in, I headed straight into my backyard, cut through it, and took refuge in Mr. Cabrera's gazebo. I fished in my backpack for my cell phone.

"Help," I said to Ana when she answered. "I need to be rescued."

"How do you know I'm not on a date?"

"Are you on a date?"

"No. S and I had a falling out."

"About?"

"His name. Besides, he never liked my mother, anyway."

"That's when she was going to be living with you. If I were him, I wouldn't like that either." My aunt Rosa had recently changed her mind about moving to town and living with Ana. Ana hadn't quite decided whether she was relieved or hurt by the decision, even though she really hadn't wanted her mother living with her.

I sympathized.

"Whose side are you on?" she asked.

"There's no sides! I'm just saying. Look, you can tell me all about it when you pick me up."

"You have perfect timing, Nina. I'm about to go on a mission. I'll be there in ten minutes. And I'm bringing the wigs."

"Oh no. Not the wigs!"

"We have to use the wigs!"

"Well, all right. But I want to be a blonde this time."

I hung up, closed my eyes, replaying what Bobby had said.

I've got something important to ask you.

I prayed he wasn't going to propose.

I didn't know how I was going to tell him no.

Eleven

"Why not marry him?" Ana asked as she drove I-75 south, toward the city.

I looked at her like she was crazy. Actually, she was crazy. It wasn't much of a stretch. "Maybe because I'm not divorced yet?"

"You will be in what? Two weeks?"

Eight days.

My stomach hurt.

"It's too soon," I said.

"Do you love him?"

Did I? I'd only known him five months. Did people fall in love in five months? "I don't know."

"I'd marry him. He's hot."

I couldn't help but laugh. "I'll keep that in mind."

"I don't like the blonde on you, Nina. You look too . . . I don't know."

I peeked in the lighted visor mirror. "Kato Kaelin?"

She banged the steering wheel with her fist. "Yes!"

"Well, it's only for one night." I sighed. "Why are we even doing this?"

"Jean-Claude, that's why."

Oh yeah. Jean-Claude.

"If he's violating his probation, then I have to take action."

Action as in sending Jean-Claude to lockup. A shame, because he only had two more months before he was a completely free man.

That made my stomach hurt too. Jean-Claude had become more than an employee to me. He was a friend.

And here I was helping to get him sent away.

But what if he's doing something dangerous? my inner voice asked.

I thought about that for a second. If he was a gigolo, as I suspected, then he was definitely doing something illegal, but dangerous? I supposed it wasn't the safest job.

And if he was stealing cars again?

Definitely dangerous. And illegal.

And not something I could condone.

I sighed. *What* was going on with him?

I wasn't happy being part of this whole bounty hunter thing Ana had going on, but as his friend, I wanted to help Jean-Claude. It was just hard to figure out what kind of help he needed.

"So," I asked, "where are we going exactly?"

"We're going to do a little recon." Ana whipped one of her long fake tresses over her shoulder.

"Recon?"

"A reconnaissance mission."

I arched an eyebrow. "You've been reading too many Tom Clancy novels."

"You know I only read sci-fi, but I did see some of those movies. Harrison Ford. Hubba hubba."

"You've got to be kidding," I said, watching headlights zip by, heading north.

"What? You like Ben Affleck?"

"Not really. But I'd take him over Harrison Ford."

Ana's face scrunched in disgust. "You've obviously been sniffing too much manure."

"Harrison Ford is old enough to be our grandfather!"

"That's only because Nana married Grandpa 'Zo when she was thirteen."

"So? Still old enough."

She held firm. "He's hot."

"Ew!"

"I also had a crush on that *Law & Order* guy. The one who just died."

I could picture his face but didn't know the name. "You're serious?"

"He was cute."

I shook my head. "This could be the root of all your failed relationships."

"Nah," she said, changing lanes. "They're cute, but not the marrying kind."

"Who is the marrying kind?"

"Your Bobby."

I groaned. This subject needed to veer off me ASAP. "What happened with you and S?"

She fidgeted. "His name."

"His name?"

"It's Shakespeare!" Her voice rose. "I can't date a guy named Shakespeare Larue!"

I pressed my lips together to keep from laughing.

"You better not be laughing!"

"Or?" A chuckle escaped.

"Argh!"

"He was a nice guy."

"I know. It's too bad."

I shook my head. "Maybe you ought to give him a second chance."

She shrugged.

I took it to mean that she'd consider a second chance if she became desperate enough—which usually happened twice a week.

"Did you get any information from Harry von Barber? Is that what this recon mission is all about?"

"I called but he didn't return it. I went to his apartment, but he wasn't there."

"Avoiding you?"

"Probably thinks I'm going to try to line him up another job with a crazy lady."

"Ha. Ha."

An eighteen wheeler rumbled past, shaking Ana's little SUV. "I went to his apartment, but he wasn't home. Luckily, his roommate, Flora, recognized the picture of Jean-Claude."

I perked up. "Oh?"

"Saw him in the Blue Zone once."

A glowing haze hovered over the city, the bright lights illuminating the night sky. The highway split off to I-71 north, and narrowed as it approached the bridge spanning the Ohio River. On the other side sat Newport, Kentucky, where we were headed.

Over the past few years, Newport had grown into a family friendly area. Newport on the Levee was a booming spot along the river that boasted boutique shops, a movie theater, restaurants, a book store, an IMAX theater, the Newport Aquarium, and amazing views of downtown Cincinnati.

Along with the growth came the Blue Zone, an upscale adult entertainment area a few blocks south of the river. The Blue Zone was a single street catering to an adult's every whim, from microbreweries to massage parlors, from fortune-tellers to a pricy sports bar where all the local pro players hung out after the game.

It was assumed that more could be attained at the massage parlors than a massage, and more than your palm could be read at the fortune-teller. I wondered if it was at one of these places that Jean-Claude worked.

"Did Flora say where she'd seen Jean-Claude?"

"He."

"Hmm?"

Ana exited the highway. "Flora's a he. I think. A very pretty he at that. I didn't ask for proof."

I turned in my seat to get a good look at her.

"Okay," she said, "I asked, but she/he didn't want to play show and tell."

"Can we trust this information?"

"Why not? It's all we've got."

True enough.

She found a place to park in an overpriced lot near the river. We hoofed it three blocks to the Blue Zone. It was clear where the nickname had come from: All the neon signs along the street were blue, casting an eerie blue glow over everything.

"Where do we start?" I asked.

She handed me a picture of Jean-Claude. It was his mug shot, the one that looked nearly identical to Hugh Grant's, which had been cropped to just see his face. "Flash that around, see what you come up with."

We split up, and I crossed the street carrying a somewhat heavy load of guilt. Because I knew that if I found Jean-Claude first, I'd probably warn him off.

If Ana found out . . .

I didn't even want to think about that. After all, she had a little bit of our Nana Ceceri's temper in her too.

The first storefront I came to was a nightclub called Bump. I waited my turn in the long line to get in, a sore thumb in my jeans and white T-shirt. Everyone else was dressed tramp-style, in microminis and barely there tube tops. Even the men had dressed skimpy, in chest clinging T-shirts and hip-hugging sleek pants. Some of them had incredible bodies.

Hey, I'm human.

When I got to the ticket booth, I held up Jean-Claude's picture. The girl, dressed head-to-toe in black—even black lipstick—motioned for me to talk to the big African-American bouncer guarding the door.

I moseyed over. "Hi."

One of his eyebrows dipped as he scanned me up and down. Then he shifted his weight—all four hundred pounds of it—and stared at me, a smirk on his face and a *no way* look in his eyes.

"Oh no," I said, "I don't want to come in."

"Good thing too. Dressed like that, you could maybe wash the dishes."

My feathers ruffled. My shoulders stiffened. Okay, so I wasn't exactly a fashion plate, but still. I held up the picture of Jean-Claude before I started a fight I'd never win. "Have you seen this man?"

The door opened behind him as someone came out of the club. Loud music with a heavy bass thumped against my ribs. The door closed, and the sound dimmed to a dull *whump, whump, whump.*

He smiled. "What's it worth to you?"

He had nice teeth, bright white and gleaming. I realized I'd been expecting gold caps, and yelled at myself for buying into stereotypes. Then it registered what he was saying. Ana hadn't mentioned anything about paying for information. In my head, I calculated what money I had. I fished in my leather backpack, pulled out my wallet.

Three fives and two ones. Not likely to buy me much. I held out a five.

He laughed.

"Ten?" I asked, pulling out another five, and giving him my best please-help-me look. I batted my eyelashes and everything.

He rolled his dark eyes, snatched the money. "That's JC."

JC. Jean-Claude. "Does he work here?"

The giant shook his head.

"Around here?"

He shrugged.

Great. I pulled out my last five.

"I've seen him at All Shook Up a few times."

"Does he work there?"

Another shrug.

I was down to my last two bucks. I figured I'd try my luck at All Shook Up. "Down that way?" I asked, pointing down the street.

The giant blew me a kiss, then brushed me aside as he let in two stunning young things with four-inch heels, mile-high legs, and way too much makeup.

In my humble opinion.

I found All Shook Up midway down the Blue Zone. It wasn't another dance club like I'd expected, but a martini bar. When I pulled open the door, I felt like I'd stepped into a zone of another sort—the Twilight Zone.

I was suddenly surrounded by Elvis. At least a hundred of them. Rhinestone jumpsuits, gold lamé, big glasses and all.

A hostess, dressed like Ann-Margret in *Viva Las Vegas,* must have caught my surprise. "Every Saturday night is Elvis night," she said. "Did you want a table?"

I shook my head, still taking in the differing Elvis hair-styles. From pompadour wigs to greased-back black dyed hair.

I held up Jean-Claude's picture. "Do you know him?"

She frowned, pulling in her bottom lip. I couldn't help but notice her breasts spilling out of the skimpy top. She'd have had no problem getting into Bump.

"He looks familiar," she said over the karaoke crooning of "Blue Moon." "Maybe ask Jake?"

"Jake?"

She pointed to a thirty-something man tending one of the three bars in the place. He too was wearing an Elvis costume.

I thanked her and started across the room. "Blue Moon" ended and someone took up the mic and started in on "Blue Suede Shoes." Sure enough, I looked down and saw that my Keds were the only white shoes in the vicinity.

I felt my phone vibrate on my hip. I flipped it open, saw Ana's name.

"Where are you?" she said.

I covered one ear with my hand, shouted, "At All Shook Up."

"Be right there!"

I slipped my phone back onto my waistband.

"Hey, baby." Elvis's hand snaked around my waist, pulling me up close and personal with his chest hair.

"Hi," I said, trying to wiggle free.

"Now now. Let's dance." The opening lines of "All Shook Up" played and the room went wild. I was definitely in the Twilight Zone.

"Really, I—"

Before I could get away, Hairy Chest had me spinning and swirling to the music. Every so often I'd look up to find him smiling at me, one corner of his mouth lifted in a classic Elvis grin.

I clutched his white jumpsuit with my left hand to keep from falling, and kept Jean-Claude's picture tight in my right hand, which was being held captive by Hairy Chest. My backpack thumped my back.

As he twirled me, I said sarcastically, "Come here often?"

He either missed the sarcasm or ignored it. "Every Saturday. You're new, though. We've got to work on your outfit. I'm thinking Joan Blackman in *Blue Hawaii*, except you'd have to go brunette."

Brunette. Right. I'd forgotten about the wig.

"Um, maybe."

The song came to a hip-jarring end. "Want a drink?" Hairy Chest asked.

More than anything. But I only had two dollars.

"My treat," he said, winking. He had pretty blue eyes, and I assumed he knew it—which was why he didn't wear those big aviator glasses like every other Elvis in the room.

"Sure." I figured he owed it to me, grabbing me like that. Though if I were really honest, I'd have to admit I'd had fun dancing. It had been a long time.

He followed me to the bar, where there were two open stools. Hairy Chest held out his hand. "Alan," he said.

"Not Elvis?"

He shrugged. He was kind of cute, and I wondered where Ana was. Maybe I could match-make while I was at this whole Jean-Claude recon thing.

Which reminded me. "Are you Jake?" I asked the bartender, just to make sure.

He winked at me, Elvis-style. I was starting to feel claustrophobic. "That's me, darlin'," he said. "Can I help you?"

After Alan and I ordered a drink, I showed him Jean-Claude's picture. "Do you know him?"

Someone started singing "Love Me Tender." Off key. I winced, wishing I'd brought ear plugs.

"Sure. That's JC. Comes in all the time."

"Really?"

"Sure. After work."

"Where's he work?"

"Can't say."

"Can't as in won't or can't as in you don't know?"

"Don't kn—"

He was cut off when I was jostled on my stool by someone sitting down next to me. It was a slightly pudgy Elvis, who would have been better off portraying an older Elvis, but had opted for a *Jailhouse Rock* look. Except he had on the glasses.

"Hey," Alan said, sticking up for me. "Watch it."

"Sorry." The Old Elvis swiveled our way.

I gasped and fell off my stool, spilling my drink down the front of my shirt.

Pudgy Elvis squinted. "Nina, is that you?" He reached down, pulled off my blonde wig, and held it out like it was something toxic.

I looked up, my mouth open, my eyes blinking as if I was hallucinating. "What are *you* doing here?"

Twelve

Hairy-chested Alan snatched my wig back, set it on my head, and helped me up. "Do you know him?" he asked me, sounding like he was looking for a fight.

I saw Pudgy Elvis take note of Alan's hands. They lingered on my bare arms. "I suggest you take your hands off of her, sonny."

"Says who, chubby?"

My father's chest puffed. I stepped in between them before punches flew. "Alan, this is my father, Antonio Ceceri. Dad, this is Alan."

My father's eyebrows, dyed freakishly black, slashed downward. "Who was just leaving, right?"

"That's up to her," Alan said, apparently having a death wish.

Just then Ana hustled in, elbowing her way through the crowd. She stopped just short of us, took in the scene. "Why do I always miss all the fun? Uncle Tonio, is that you?"

My father murmured something under his breath, ordered a drink from Jake.

Alan took one look at Ana and lost interest in me. I sat down next to my father while a female Elvis took the karaoke mic and started singing "In the Ghetto." She was booed off the stage.

"Do I even want to know?" I asked my father, dabbing at the front of my shirt with a cocktail napkin. The outline of my pink Victoria's Secret bra was clearly visible for all to see. "Mom thinks you're at some club meeting or something."

He picked up his shot glass. "This is one of the club's outings."

"What kind of club are you in? It's certainly not Historians Unite, or whatever Mom told me."

My father's chest puffed again. "It's called 'Elvis Lives.' We meet twice a month and come here every Saturday night. And your mother knows what I'm doing. She just doesn't want to admit it."

I could see why. "Does that goop come out?" I motioned to his eyebrows. I didn't even mention the pitch-black toupee. I had my limits.

"All water soluble."

"Ah."

"Am I really chubby?" he asked, running a hand over his stomach.

"In a good way," I said. "Think Santa."

He frowned, took another sip of his drink.

Over my shoulder I saw Alan give Ana his phone number. She put it in her pocket and sat on the other side of my father. Alan headed for the karaoke line.

"Uncle Tonio," Ana said, "you look cool!"

He kissed both her cheeks. "Am I fat?" he asked her.

"In a good way," she said.

My father grunted.

"See, I told you so." I wanted to order another drink but didn't want to have to borrow money. I asked for water instead.

"You're Italian," Ana said, as if this explained everything

from chubbiness to the Darwin Theory. She then leaned across the bar top and said to me, "Did you find him?"

"Him who?" my father asked.

"Jean-Claude," Ana said to him.

"Who's Jean-Claude?" he asked.

I picked up another napkin, kept dabbing. "He works for me, remember?"

My father shook his head, the weird toupee flapping.

I dabbed harder.

"Well, Nina thought he might have been a prostitute."

"A gigolo," I corrected. I looked up at Jake, who was hovering. "That's right, right? Girls are prostitutes, men are gigolos?"

"I think both prefer 'escorts' these days," he said.

My father made the sign of the cross.

"Well, we're not sure he's any of those," Ana said. "He's moonlighting but we don't know where."

"Do we care?" my father asked.

Ana ordered something I'd never heard of before. "He could be violating his probation."

"Ah."

I told Ana about my trip to Bump. She laughed about the fifteen dollars. "I'm surprised you got any information about Jean-Claude with only fifteen bucks."

Jake set Ana's drink down. It was pink with a little umbrella. "Oh, is this about JC again?" he asked, looking at Ana's copy of Jean-Claude's mug shot.

"Who's JC?" Ana asked.

"Jean-Claude," I explained.

"Since when does he go by JC?" she asked.

"I've only known him as JC." Jake swiped the countertop. "His real name is Jean-Claude?"

"Does anyone, perchance, have an aspirin?" my father asked.

I fished in my backpack and pulled out a tin of Advil.

"Jean-Claude Reaux."

Jake put another stack of napkins in front of me. "I know him as JC Rock."

"JC Rock?" Ana laughed, tossing her head back. The curls of her red wig flounced.

"Do I want to ask about the wigs?" my father asked.

I gave up on my shirt. "Only if you want us to ask about yours."

He pressed his lips together, signaled for a refill to his Jim Beam.

"Do you know where he works?" Ana asked Jake, switching back to the topic of Jean-Claude.

"No, but he comes in almost every Saturday night." He looked at his watch. "Usually around three."

"Three? A.M.?"

"What?" Ana said to me, "too late for you?"

"Don't give me that." I slid my water glass in circles, wishing it were something pink with an umbrella in it. "It's past your bedtime too."

My father said, "Don't look at me. One o'clock is my limit."

Ana and I looked at Jake. "Want to do a little recon?" I asked.

He set the bar rag over his shoulder. "Like a Tom Clancy novel?"

"Exactly," Ana said.

We explained what we wanted to know, and Jake promised he'd try to get the information for us in exchange for a date with Ana.

My ego was bruised, but I was glad we were finally going to find out what Jean-Claude was up to.

"Speaking of Tom Clancy," Ana said to Jake, "who do

you think was better in those movies? Harrison Ford or Ben Affleck?"

Someone sang "A Little Less Conversation" as Jake said, "Harrison Ford. Everyone knows that."

I woke up the next morning to a ringing sound and Ana thumping my head like it was the snooze button of her alarm clock.

I lifted a heavy eyelid and searched for a clock. It was ten in the morning. The ringing continued, and I wondered if I had a hangover.

Then I remembered I'd only had one drink—barely.

"Phone," Ana mumbled, pulling a pillow over her head.

My cell phone, I realized with a start. I rolled out of Ana's bed, stumbled toward my backpack, which was still buzzing. I found my phone, flipped it open, and mumbled something in the way of a greeting. I think it might have been "Hello" but may have come out as "Yo."

"Sleeping late, are we?"

I padded into Ana's living room, flopped onto her sofa, and drew a chenille throw over my bare legs. I'd borrowed one of Ana's T-shirts and a pair of boxer shorts—I didn't want to know their origin—to sleep in.

"Good morning to you too. You never were a morning person," I said.

Kevin grunted. "It's practically afternoon. Loverboy tire you out?"

I ground my teeth, rubbed the sleep from my eyes. "No, Ana tires me out. She hogs the covers."

Banging my head with my fist, I wondered why I'd said anything at all. Why did I care if he thought I'd slept with Bobby?

Why? We. Were. Over.

Done.

Finito.

Right?

Ugh.

"But your mother . . . Never mind," he said.

Ah. My mother probably assumed I'd changed my mind last night and gone home with Bobby after all. Probably I should have told her I was going out with Ana and that I'd decided to stay the night at her place. I'm sure my father had filled her in by now.

"Earth to Nina" I heard in my ear.

"What?"

"Talk about not being a morning person."

"Is Riley okay? Is that why you're calling?"

I yawned. Doing recon took its toll.

"He's fine," Kevin said. "I just dropped him off at work. Can you pick him up?"

"Sure."

"Great. All right, I've got good news and bad news. Which do you want first?"

"Good," I said. I could use a pick-me-up.

"The Grabinsky yard has been cleared. As soon as you get the go-ahead from Greta Grabinsky you can finish the job there."

Oh, like that was going to be easy.

I debated whether I should tell him about the conversation in Greta's kitchen I'd overheard. Decided it was the right thing to do. Taking a deep breath, I told Kevin about the threats.

"And how do you know about these threats?" he asked. I heard irritation in his voice.

"I, um, told you. I overheard."

"And where were you?"

"Ah, um, in the Grabinskys' yard?"

"Nina . . ." he warned.

I sat upright, getting tangled in the chenille blanket. "I've, um, got to go."

"Wait!"

I winced, bracing for the worst.

"We can hash out the whole trespassing thing later, not to mention crossing a crime scene line." He sighed. "The bad news . . ."

I'd forgotten about the bad news. My heart sank down to the pit of my stomach. "Do I want to know?"

"You have to know."

"What is it?"

His voice dropped to a whisper, as though he didn't want to be overheard. "I shouldn't be telling you this."

I didn't know what to say to that, so I kept quiet.

"The captain, well, he's looking to make a case with the prosecutor's office."

"What kind of case?"

"There was a case in New Jersey recently where a man died of a heart attack because he'd been scared to death at a bank robbery."

"Meaning?"

"Meaning that the prosecutor's office is looking into charging someone with murder for Russ Grabinsky's death."

"Someone as in me?"

"You and the Lockharts."

"Even if it was a heart attack?"

"Even if. It's like what that annoying HOA lady was saying the other day. He might have died from the shock of it all. Look, the prosecutor is desperate to make a name for himself, Nina. You know the problems the department has had lately, so the captain is bending over backward to help him."

There had been some rumblings over the past six months in the department of briberies and kickbacks, rumors of bad cops. Nothing had ever come of it, and the prosecutor ended up looking like a fool.

"I was just doing my job!"

"Nina, calm down. I'm just saying it's being talked about. And it probably wouldn't be murder charges. Maybe man one, or involuntary manslaughter."

"Oh, that makes me feel much better."

"I just wanted to let you know."

"Thanks," I mumbled and hung up the phone.

"You okay?" Ana asked from the doorway.

I looked up at her. "If I get probation, will you find a good job for me?"

Thirteen

I was afraid to go home, but since I didn't have any clean clothes, I didn't have a choice.

Ana had done her best to cheer me up, but at ten on a Sunday Ana is not at her best. Especially since she'd had many more drinks than I did last night.

Ana dropped me off and drove away before I even made it to the front steps. I didn't blame her. She knew my mother was inside and assumed my father had filled her in on our foray into the Blue Zone. She didn't want the lecture any more than I did.

Unfortunately I didn't have a choice.

Ana really didn't either. She was just delaying the inevitable. My mother had a long memory and would undoubtedly bring up this situation the next time she saw her.

The front door flew open before my foot hit the porch. "*Chérie!* How was it?" She waggled her eyebrows.

It took me a second to process what she was saying. "Good?" I hedged.

Maybe my father hadn't spoken to her yet . . . Maybe she still thought I'd spent the night with Bobby . . .

"Are you asking *me, chérie*?"

I decided to keep her in the dark. For now. "No, no. It was

good." Fantasies of me and Bobby in bed played in my mind. "Really good."

I stepped into the house, preparing for the worst. I'd seen some of those home improvement shows and their nightmare results.

Oh, not all of them were disastrous, but Maria had had orange paint on her. Orange.

Dear Lord.

Paint fumes lingered in the air, but as I looked around, I didn't see any evidence of paint. I looked at my mother. "What room did you change?"

"Upstairs. Were there candles? I love when your father lights a lot of can—"

"Eww! Stop!"

"What?"

"I don't want to talk about this."

"Why? I am your mamá! You can talk to me about everything."

Except that. I shuddered. "Where's Maria?"

"Shopping."

Ah.

"Want to see your room?" she asked me, her face lighting.

Orange. I sucked it up. "Sure."

She latched onto my hand, her skin smooth. Time had been kind to her. Barely any wrinkles marred her creamy white complexion. Maria was the spitting image of her, with blonde hair, blue eyes, and a natural grace.

I took after my father. And after seeing him last night, I was beginning to worry how I'd turn out.

"You're all tense," my mother said, looking back at me as we climbed the stairs. "Are you all right?"

"I'm fine." I didn't want to worry her with the whole Grabinsky thing. Not until there was something to worry about. "Late night," I said.

When my mother broke into a smile, I realized it had been the wrong thing to say. I fully expected another maternal interrogation, and was surprised when she didn't ask any questions. She simply said, "I'm happy for you, *chérie*."

I swallowed over a sudden lump in my throat and fought off tears. She, at times, could say just the right thing.

She patted my hand. "You can have all day to rest."

I wished I could. I needed to speak with Greta Grabinsky. I also had work to do. TBS was open on Sundays for a half day. Usually it was time to meet with clients, catch up on paperwork, but today there was a mini going on. Deanna's first, planned solo.

She had the confidence and know-how to pull it off, but I wanted to at least pop in at the site and give her encouragement and support.

I also needed to call Bobby to plan when we could get together. To talk.

"Come, come," my mother said. "I cannot wait for you to see your room."

Worried, I held my breath as she pushed open my door.

"Ta-da!"

All I could do was stare. And stare some more.

Gone was my standard, no muss no fuss bed. Gone were the two dressers, one still empty in Kevin's absence. The paint had gone from a bland white to a creamy yellow.

No orange!

My inner self did a happy dance.

I walked in, absorbing.

A queen-size canopy bed angled in the corner took up most of the space. The canopy was made of white flowing gauze material. The bed looked heavenly with a mile high feather bed, thick ivory down comforter, and tons of pillows. Hints of cranberry color popped up here and there. In the pillows on the bed, on the lamp on the bedside table, in the throw rugs on my new hardwood floor.

I blinked.

Hardwood?

"Did you do all this yourselves?"

My mother winked. "We had help."

"It's so beautiful."

She clapped, reminding me again of Maria. "We knew you'd like it!"

I never would have thought I'd like something so feminine, but it appealed to a side of me I rarely indulged. This was so perfect. For so many reasons. The biggest being that it helped to erase the memories of Kevin from this room.

"I don't know what to say."

"There's no need to say anything. You do for so many, *chérie*. It was time someone did for you."

"Thank you, Mom, it's beautiful."

And I couldn't help but think I wanted to show it to Bobby as soon as possible.

As I spun, taking in the little details, the touches of wrought iron, the new crown molding, I caught a glimpse of my adjoining bathroom and noticed that the seventies era flowered wallpaper wasn't up anymore.

"Did you do the bathroom too?" I asked, amazed. I started forward to get a better look.

My mother dashed in front of me, blocked the entrance.

I hadn't known she could move so fast. Usually she walked with a slow casualness that drove me nuts.

"Um, well—" My mother rarely stuttered. "We thought it needed updating also."

I tried to peer over her shoulder. "Anything is better than Aunt Chi-Chi's old wallpaper."

It had truly been hideous, teal and navy flowers.

"Yes, well . . ."

I stood on tiptoes, suddenly suspicious. "What's wrong?"

"Wrong? What could be wrong?"

"I don't know. You're the one who won't let me see."

She brushed a lock of blonde hair off her forehead, swept it back with a practiced grace. "It's simply not done yet."

I made a move to peek over her shoulder, but ducked at the last minute under her rigid arm and pushed my way into my bathroom.

Or what was left of my bathroom.

"Oh. My."

"It's not so bad, *chérie*."

I looked around at the big gaping holes in my walls. Everything was . . .

Worthy of a state of emergency declaration.

The tub was pulled away from the wall, the showerhead and tiles gone. My vanity sat in the middle of the floor, which no longer had any linoleum on it. The sink was filled with dust, and the plumbing, the pipes, and doodads I didn't know the names of stuck out of the wall.

"What happened?" I asked.

"It all started with the wallpaper. It tore the plaster from the wall when we took it off. The plasterer we called told us it wasn't worth restoring and suggested we gut it and replace it with drywall. The demo crew will be here tomorrow."

The demo crew. Here. Tomorrow.

"When will they be done?"

"Good things are worth waiting for, *chérie*."

Ugh!

Absently, I wondered who was paying for all this, and decided I'd jump that hurdle later.

For now, my thoughts of a hot relaxing shower vanished faster than Riley when I'd brought up the topic of safe sex.

"Don't look so forlorn. There is another bathroom in the house."

Riley's.

I shuddered.

Forcing myself to remember that my mother had only been trying to do something nice for me, I mustered up a smile. "I'm sure it will look really nice."

She kissed both my cheeks, yawned and said, "I'm going home now."

To see my father. Who'd undoubtedly fill her in on my nighttime adventure.

I saw her off, called Maria and left a thank-you message on her voice mail, and quickly took a shower in Riley's bathroom, trying not to feel displaced.

The phone rang as I was slipping into a clean pair of shorts.

"Hey," Bobby said.

I sighed. I couldn't help myself. His voice did that to me. It was a totally feminine reaction I hated, but it wasn't to be helped. And it almost—almost—made me forget all about my legal problems and construction woes.

"Hi," I said.

"Sleep well?"

Well enough considering Ana hogged covers and tended to throw elbows while she slept.

But he didn't need to know all that right now. I'd fill him in later. "Good. You?"

"I was lonely," he said in a way that heated my blood.

For some reason, I kept hearing faint strains of "Are You Lonesome Tonight" in my head. "Oh?"

"Is that all I get? An 'oh'?"

I should maybe tell him how I'd had to sit down because my knees had gone weak at the thoughts of me and him, him and me in my new bed. "It's a good oh," I said.

"Is there such a thing?"

"Definitely."

I heard a smile in his voice as he said, "I'll keep that in mind. How's your schedule?" he asked. "Is lunch a possibility?"

I've got something important to ask you.

I chewed a fingernail.

"Nina?"

I'd have to deal with it sooner or later. Might as well be sooner. Right?

I eyed my fingernails, looking for a jagged edge. Sooner just wasn't working for me. I needed a little more time. "I've actually got to work this afternoon." Which was true, so I didn't feel the least bit guilty.

Okay, a little guilty.

"How about dinner?"

Dinner sometimes led to dessert. And nightcaps. And big fluffy beds. "Sounds good."

We agreed to a time, and I hung up, feeling slightly queasy yet excited at the same time. I knew I had to head into work, but if I was to be using Riley's bathroom for the foreseeable future, it needed to be cleaned. Scrubbed, actually.

As I gathered up supplies, I couldn't help but remember that cleaning the bathrooms had been Kevin's household chore. I'd loved that about him.

Loved.

Love?

Don't think about it, I told myself. Over and over.

I threw myself into scrubbing, trying to figure out what to do about Greta Grabinsky.

Did she want me to finish the yard or not? In her current state of mind, I'd have to say no. But if a foreclosure lawsuit was pending, did she have a choice?

Had the lawsuit been dropped as the man in her kitchen

insinuated? I wondered how I could find out, and decided to check with Kate Hathaway, the Fallow Falls HOA president. She'd know one way or another.

Thank goodness I'd already been paid for the job.

No refunds.

Not that I could see Bill and Lindsey asking for one. Not after all they put me through.

I'd decided not to sue them unless I was sued by Greta. Unlike the Fallow Falls community, I wasn't lawsuit happy.

But I could hold a grudge. And I did against the Lockharts. They'd out and out used me.

But hadn't you used them? my inner voice asked.

No.

Maybe.

Kinda-sorta.

Okay, so I'd wanted to know about Kevin's first wife . . . That wasn't a crime. I'd still planned to do a good job for them.

And look where it'd landed me. With a pending lawsuit, possible murder charges, and no information—nada, zip, nothing—on Leah Quinn.

I finished the bathroom, tidied up, locked the house. As I backed out of my driveway on my way to work, I saw Mr. Cabrera watering his flower beds. Boom-Boom sat on his front step, keeping him company.

She apparently hadn't heard about Mr. Cabrera's curse yet. Brickhouse would be thrilled to pieces.

Speaking of Brickhouse, I needed to mentally prepare myself for her gloating. I'd planned to visit Tam sometime during the day. I couldn't imagine it was any fun being in the hospital all day with nothing to do. And though she and Ian were now living together, she didn't have any family in the area. Thankfully, I had plenty to spare, and I made a quick call to my mother, who would have Tam surrounded by lasagnas and bear hugs before sunset.

TBS was locked tight when I got there. The chimes still hung from the door, but they didn't sound as harmonious as before. I plucked a boxwood stem from one of the pipes and went to check my messages.

There were six from Deanna, who apparently was having a panic attack over her solo job today. Thankfully, Kit would be there to keep her sane.

As I popped open a Dr Pepper, I wondered if Deanna really had a crush on Kit or if she was just playing with him. I hoped it was the latter, because Deanna was young and sweet and I didn't want her to have a broken heart.

I sat at my desk, answered relevant e-mails, deleted spam, except for the ad for hair growth, which I forwarded to Kit's e-mail. He'd appreciate the joke, I was sure.

For an hour I returned phone calls from clients and potential clients. Apparently the dead guy on the news hadn't hurt business too much, but I had to wonder what the fallout would be from Greta's potential lawsuit and the murder charges.

On a whim, I picked up the phone and called Lindsey Lockhart to see if she'd had any luck convincing Greta not to sue. She seemed surprised to hear from me, though I couldn't imagine why.

It wasn't every day someone tricked me into doing a backyard makeover for someone else.

"Nina, I'm so sorry about everything that happened. Greta's just grief-stricken. When she comes to her senses she'll understand."

"Have you talked with her?"

"Well, no. I tried, but she wouldn't open the door."

I drew my thumb along the edge of my desk.

Would Greta change her mind? She'd seemed more angry than grief-stricken to me, and I wondered again what kind of marriage she and Russ had had. And asked.

"They'd been married a long time, Nina. Everyone has problems when you've been married forty years."

"Forty years? Really?"

A daddy longlegs crawled along the windowsill. I rolled my chair over to the window, opened it, and helped Daddy outside. He didn't make it, but instead started crawling up the screen.

"She was eighteen when they married. She'd been an apprentice bookkeeper at a shoe shop and he was her boss. Love at first sight, Greta told me."

"How much older was he than her?"

I heard faint music playing in the background. "Ten years."

That was a big gap when one of them was only eighteen. She'd probably just gotten out of school. Gone from her parents' house to Russ's.

"I keep hearing how unkind he was. Was he unkind to Greta too?"

"She never said."

"But you suspected, right? Isn't that why you and Bill did the makeover? To help her because Russ wouldn't?"

Lindsey sighed. "He treated her like a possession. Very controlling. Whenever she did something for herself, he criticized and belittled. The homeowners' association, for example."

"Oh?"

"Greta wanted to join because she figured it would spur Russ to do something about the yard. Only he thought it was ridiculous and refused to pay the dues or listen to the notices. On principle, he'd said. I think it was because he was cheap."

"Why didn't she leave him?" I asked.

"Simple. She loved him."

Over and over again I kept replaying the rumor I'd heard the day Russ died.

I heard his wife was hoping he'd have a heart attack when he saw the yard. That's why she hired these people.

Was there any truth to it?

No, simply because Greta hadn't planned the makeover. Bill and Lindsey had.

As the daddy longlegs scampered up the screen, looking for a way out, I thought about that.

Had *they* wanted Russ dead? Could *that* have been the true motive behind the makeover? Not the lawsuit, which was the line Bill and Lindsey had fed me, but something much more sinister?

After all, Lindsey and Bill had known about Russ's bad heart. Had they planned the makeover hoping he'd have a heart attack from the surprise?

They'd known how he felt about the HOA. They'd had to have known his reaction to a total backyard makeover.

And anticipated it?

A chill ran up my spine as the daddy longlegs found a hole in the screen and crawled to freedom.

Maybe I'd been reading too much Tom Clancy. All this subterfuge and backstabbing seemed much better suited to a spy novel.

"I just need to talk to Greta," Lindsey said. "Get her to see reason. We were trying to help her, not harm her."

Or were they? I couldn't dismiss the fact that they'd both known about Russ's bad heart. Throw in a surprise makeover and it's a perfect recipe for heart attack.

"Whose idea was it? To do the makeover, I mean?"

I heard the low hum of a country music station come across the line, louder now in her silence. "I'm just not sure. Let me think."

I let her, drumming my fingers on my stained desk blotter. Finally she said, "You know, it was Bill. Right after Riley came to work for him. Bill was excited about helping Greta."

I bet. Especially if he wanted Russ dead.

I knew I was jumping to conclusions.

"But twenty thousand dollars is awfully generous. Don't you think?"

"I had sticker shock for a month, but Bill was adamant we had to do this for Greta. And for Russ too. We just knew he'd appreciate it once he set his pride aside."

"Why Russ? I thought the whole lawsuit thing was his fault."

"Well, Russ took a chance on Bill, trusting him with Growl, to get it going, make it successful." She laughed. "And he did that, plus some."

It was true. Growl was flourishing, garnering all sorts of great press as an innovative, affordable, healthy alternative to the big burger places.

Yet . . . "Trust him? Isn't Bill a co-owner? Fifty-fifty? Didn't he have as much to lose as Russ if Growl failed?"

"Not at first. It was seventy-five, twenty-five," Lindsey said. "We couldn't afford to go in halfway right off. It wasn't until last year that we could buy out the other twenty-five percent."

It sounded to me as if there was a soft side to Russ no one ever got to see. Especially if he'd taken a chance with Bill.

But I couldn't help but wonder if it had been a mistake to trust Bill Lockhart. There was just something about him that put me off.

Maybe it was because I'd never go spending twenty thousand dollars out of the goodness of my heart.

Who had that kind of money to throw around?

Had Russ? Would he have done the same if the situation were reversed?

I thought back to differences between the Grabinskys' house and the Lockharts'. Bill and Lindsey's said money all the way down to the hanging baskets and freshly painted trim on their house, while the Grabinskys' had rusting wrought-iron railings and tattered throw blankets.

Hmm.

Had Russ really been an Ebenezer? Or could it be that Bill was fiddling with the books?

The accounting books!

I bolted out of my chair, nearly choking myself on the telephone cord. Russ had taken the account books home—and Bill desperately wanted them back.

Coincidence?

I had a strict commandment not to believe in coincidences.

I wasn't about to go breaking it now.

Quickly saying my good-byes, I hung up and looked at my watch. I needed to get over to Deanna's mini before she finished. Then I wanted to go see Greta Grabinsky. Maybe even get a peek at those books while I tried to talk her out of suing me.

Fourteen

I searched for a parking spot near the Sandruzzis' house and finally found one down the block, behind an unmarked TBS truck.

The Sandruzzis were a young, married, double income couple, and it was Amy Sandruzzi's birthday. In addition to a huge surprise party, her husband Darryl had hired TBS. The mini was actually taking place in the front yard, sprucing up lackluster curb appeal.

As I walked along the street's edge—there were no sidewalks in this older part of town—I could see that the makeover was just about done.

I stood between a parked minivan and a TBS pickup, taking it all in. The house was a traditional ranch, center entrance, low roof. Nothing too exciting, but in good condition. It had been recently painted a soft yellow, much like my new bedroom.

Which got me thinking about my bed.

And Bobby in it.

And that I was meeting him tonight.

So we could talk.

Ack.

I pushed that out of my mind and focused on the Sandruzzis' yard transformation.

Deanna had done an excellent job. Her design had included tearing out the old concrete walkway and replacing it with a new brick one, painting the concrete landing, and bordering the now curving path with flower beds on each side.

Beautiful bright-leafed coleus and bluish purple fanflowers glowed against fresh mulch. Japanese holly bushes, an evergreen shrub with small shiny leaves, and rhododendrons—the evergreen Lee's dark purple—added to the visual appeal. To the right of the front door Deanna had added a trellis between two single hung windows, and a clematis had been planted at its base, its spindly fingers already searching for something to grab onto. Under the family room's large picture window Deanna had added a long window box, filled with blue wave petunias. Just petunias. Against the yellow background, the simplicity was stunning.

The front bushes, old overgrown Japanese yews, had been removed and three burning bushes planted in a neat row.

To the left of the walkway a young crabapple had been planted. The same brick as the walkway had been used to create a circular planting bed around the crabapple, where yellow zinnias and dahlias along with a mixture of pink, red, rose, white, and yellow snapdragons added color and interest. To my eye, the only work left was some mulching around the fire bushes and cleanup.

"Nina! Look out!"

My head snapped up and I saw a big black blur barreling down on me.

BeBe!

I scrambled onto the back bumper of the pickup and hurled myself into its bed.

Two dinner plate-sized paws landed on top of the tailgate, and BeBe's head appeared, drool dripping from her big lolling tongue.

Marty, panting and out of breath, grabbed BeBe's leash, but couldn't get her to budge.

BeBe strained, scratching the tailgate.

Reluctantly, I gave in and stuck out my hand. BeBe started licking it like it was a T-bone flavored doggy popsicle.

Ew!

"Kit!" I yelled.

Kit's chin snapped up. He'd been working on the mulch. His fuzzy head swiveled, and I lip-read the swear that came out of his mouth as he took in the situation.

I caught his gaze, shot daggers at him. Sharp ones.

For a second he looked like he wanted to run. He didn't like angry women. He'd have to get over that.

BeBe continued to slobber as Kit hurried over. Marty had finally caught his breath and said to me, "Sorry, Nina. If I'd known you were coming, I'd have kept a tighter hold on her. She must have smelled you or something."

My hand dripped drool. I'd finally had enough and pulled it away, wiping it down my shorts.

There wasn't enough degerminator in the world.

"What's she doing here?" I asked Kit, not too nicely.

BeBe tried to jump into the truck bed with me. Kit tugged her leash away from Marty and gave him a dirty look.

"What?" Marty said. "BeBe must have smelled Nina or something. She just took off all of a sudden."

"I wish you'd stop saying I smell!"

"If the deodorant fits," Kit said.

"Ha. Ha." If he didn't look so little boylike with his fuzzy head and long, drooping eyelashes, he'd be dead meat. "Don't try to evade. What's BeBe doing here?"

"Daisy got a new job. Crazy hours."

I couldn't help myself. Discreetly I took a sniff of my armpits and caught a whiff of Secret's Mountain Glade. Maybe BeBe had Secret fetish?

I folded my arms across my chest, felt some residual BeBe drool. I needed another shower. "What kind of job?" All right, I was being nosy, but I couldn't help myself.

"She's in medicine."

BeBe woofed. She apparently wanted some more Ninacicle, as her tongue hung over the tailgate, slurping air.

I forced myself not to get distracted (but who knew dogs had such long tongues?). "What kind of medicine?"

"Pharmaceuticals."

There was a whole range of areas that covered, from prescription to recreational.

I decided not to press.

Looking up at the sound of pounding footsteps, I saw Deanna bearing down, a clipboard tucked under her outstretched arm, her watch glinting in the sunlight. With her right hand she tapped the watch face.

"People! Deadlines!" When she spotted me, she smiled and said, "What do you think?"

Nothing about me being hunkered in the back of the pickup. Oh, no, nothing unusual about that.

But I supposed she had a lot on her mind.

"I think it's beautiful," I said. "You did a great job."

Her cheeks reddened with the praise and she smiled like a proud new mother. "Thanks," she said, then became all business again by turning and tapping her watch and saying, "People! People! Amy Sandruzzi will be home in twenty minutes. That means you too, Kit."

I didn't think I had to worry about Deanna having a crush on Kit anymore. Not with that tone.

"You better go," I said to him.

He tugged on BeBe's leash and actually got her to heel.

I caught his eye. "No more BeBe, Kit."

A dark eyebrow slashed upward. "Or what?"

I supposed he was trying for menacing, but I knew him too well. And the whole eyebrow thing looked more comical than dangerous. I bit my lip, but the laugh came out.

"What?" he asked, a frown pulling his thin lips downward.

" 'Or else,' " I mocked.

His jaw set. "It's the hair, isn't it? No one takes me seriously with this fuzz on my head."

"It doesn't help," I said, raising my hand to wipe away the tears from my eyes, but then stopped because I remembered BeBe's slobber. I used the neck of my T-shirt instead.

Offended, Kit spun and sauntered away, BeBe trying her best to get back to me the whole time.

I glanced at my watch, saw that if I wanted to stop by Greta's house, I needed to get going. Riley was expecting me to pick him up soon. I climbed out of the pickup bed, took one last look at the Sandruzzi yard. It was in good hands.

I felt like a proud mama.

I parked my truck in front of the Grabinsky house and sat there for a minute.

The more involved I became with this whole mess, the more I regretted ever signing on to do the job.

Right then and there I made a commandment to not be so nosy where Kevin's first wife was concerned.

It was none of my business.

Now that it was a commandment, I'd have to stick to it. I'd yet to find a loophole where commandments were concerned.

Lindsey and Bill's explanation of why they hired me made sense on the surface . . .

But every time I repeated it, I kind of had that feeling I got after eating a whole roll of cookie dough.

All queasy, nothing sitting well.

"I don't buy it."

There, I said it. I didn't believe Lindsey and Bill. Not one bit. There's just no way, neighborly love or not, that someone would dole out that kind of money—and I charged a lot—for a gift. Especially since I knew Bill and Russ didn't get along all that well.

Murder made much more sense.

"Eee!" I screamed when someone knocked on my passenger window. Turning, I found Meredith Adams, HOA VP, staring at me, arms folded, severely plucked eyebrows arched, sadistic smile gleaming.

Gritting my teeth, I powered down the window, then rubbed the spot on the top of my leg where it hit on the steering wheel when I'd jumped.

Bulging eyes narrowed. "There is no loitering allowed in this neighborhood."

"Did you have a horrible childhood?"

The smile faded. Her lips pursed as though she'd just tried some of Ana's cooking. "Move along or I will be forced to call the authorities."

I was sure she'd love that. The rebellious part of me wanted to sit here all day long. But I had things to do, Riley to pick up, and a date with Bobby tonight.

Bobby. Sigh.

"I will, you know."

"What? Leave your poor eyebrows alone next time?"

She huffed. "Call the authorities. I have the right. I have the power."

"Meredith, you need help." I decided not to waste any more of my time with her, got out of the truck and walked away, up to Greta's front door. I had the feeling if I turned around, Meredith would still be standing there, waiting to do battle.

I didn't turn. I didn't want to give her the satisfaction.

I knocked instead. No sound came from inside, so I leaned over the railing and peeked in the front window. Nothing had changed since the last time I'd done so. Everything was in place, from the afghan to the accounting books.

Oh, how I itched to go through them.

I rang the bell.

Still nothing from inside.

"No one's seen her since yesterday," a soft voice said.

I almost fell down the stairs. What was it with people sneaking up on me lately?

Kate Hathaway stood at the bottom of the steps. "Sorry," she said. "I didn't mean to startle you. I saw Meredith huffing and puffing at the curb, saw your truck, and decided I better come out before you very justifiably run her over."

I smiled. I liked Kate. "Thanks."

"I'm sorry about all this lawsuit business. I just feel terrible you were drawn into it."

Coming down the steps, I noticed Meredith had disappeared. I breathed a sigh of relief because, honestly, running her over had gone through my head.

More than once.

"I just think if I can explain to Greta . . ."

"She's stubborn, just like Russ was. I think that's why she stayed with him so long."

Kate wore a soft orange-colored halter top, loose and flowing, with white capris. A gold link anklet encircled her right ankle, and she was barefoot. I liked her even more. I was a barefoot kind of girl at heart.

Stubborn? Or scared? The thought of leaving after forty years of depending on someone else had to be terrifying. Not to mention that by all accounts, Russ was an abuser. Mentally, definitely, but physically too?

"I hear he was horrible."

She scrunched her nose. "I don't like to speak badly about the dead, but honestly? He was the worst."

"Was the homeowners' lawsuit designed to get him out of the neighborhood?"

"I'm not going to lie. It would have been an added benefit. But you saw the yard. It was an eyesore, and in definite violation of our codes."

I could see why she had been voted president of the homeowners' association. She had an easy way about her, but under the pretty surface, she was smart. I imagined she got what she wanted—a lot.

"Codes the HOA designed specifically because of him?" I asked.

She shrugged. "It's a standard agreement."

"Was he mad when he found out Greta joined the HOA without his permission?"

"Fuming. Wouldn't pay dues or respond to our notices. We had no choice but to file a suit against him."

"But I heard the suit had been dropped."

"Dropped?"

"That's what I heard." I didn't tell her where.

"From whom?"

I really couldn't say since I didn't know the identity of the man in Greta's kitchen. "It's not true?"

"No," she said. "It's not."

So, had Greta's visitor been lying? It seemed that way, without a doubt.

"Where did you hear it?"

I hedged. "Somewhere. I can't place it."

"Well, if you do, please let me know."

"I will. And if you happen to see Greta, would you please let her know I need to talk to her? I can't finish the job in her backyard without her permission. And right now she's refusing to speak to me."

Kate's eyes widened.

"You seem concerned."

"Well, as it is, the yard is still an eyesore."

It really was, all torn up, yard debris everywhere. I cringed because I hated leaving a job undone.

"Despite what you heard, the homeowner association's lawsuit is still in effect, Ms. Quinn."

"Nina, please. And what does that mean?"

"It means that Greta has until the end of the month to repay the dues and to have the yard fixed or the house will be foreclosed upon."

"Does she know this? What if she's under the impression the suit has been dropped?"

"I'll have the lawyers get in touch with her again. Now that Russ is out of the picture, I can't imagine there being any issues or that she'd follow through with her threats to sue you. She needs you if she wants to save her house."

That made me feel better.

As I drove away I slowed in front of the Lockharts' house. There was a small SUV in the driveway that had a local real estate agent's logo on it. I pulled up to the curb as a woman pulled a For Sale sign out of the hatchback.

I leaned out the passenger window. "Excuse me, is this house for sale?"

She perked right up, sensing a sale. "Officially on the market tomorrow."

Interestinger and interestinger.

"Really? It's such a lovely house. I can't imagine anyone moving from it? Was it a job transfer?"

She came up to my window. "No, just not enough space for the family anymore."

My foot.

"They're actually moving into Vista View . . . heard of it?"

I knew it quite well. It was a neighborhood of half-million- to multi-million-dollar homes.

Bill and Lindsey were movin' on up.

Now that they could afford it? Because Russ was dead?

I thanked the agent, who looked put out that I didn't make an appointment to look at the house, and headed toward Growl thinking that the motives for killing Russ were stacking up against Bill.

Fifteen

Growl had been in business for about a year now, and doing quite well as far as I knew. The parking lot was almost full when I pulled in. The building was a modern design, all sleek lines and dark stone. In a former life it had been an upscale coffeehouse.

I wondered if Bill was working. And if I could find out more information about those accounting books.

Inside, the place was jumping. I looked around for Riley and found him at a register, taking orders. He looked awfully cute in his dress shirt and nice pants, both black. Not that I'd ever tell him so. He still got defensive about those kinds of things.

He spotted me and held up a wait-a-minute finger. I took the opportunity to look around, see if I could spot Bill.

There were three registers in use, and a mix of patrons ranged from young gen-exers fresh from the office, to scrubby looking teens, to senior citizens looking for a discount. I spotted two vegetarian T-shirts. The majority of people seemed to be in their twenties and thirties, business types if the suits and sensible shoes were any indication.

Growl had accomplished what many other places hadn't—bridging the age gap and closing the financial divide.

The lines were long, yet people didn't look impatient. Someone walked by me with a tray of food that smelled heavenly but looked horrible. Too many green and slimy things on the plate. Spinach, I think. And some marinated mushrooms.

Yuck!

I glanced up at the menu. It was divided into three sections. Soups, salads, entrées. The soups made me shudder. Stuff like Asparagus Delight, which was an oxymoron if I ever heard one, Lentil Stew, Split Pea, Mushroom Barley, Forest Mushroom. I shuddered.

I'm sorry, but anything grown in a forest should stay in a forest. My gaze moved onto the salad menu. If I were a salad person, it wouldn't be too bad. There was Dandelion Green Salad, Mandarin Spinach Salad, Portabella Mushroom Salad, and Vegetarian Antipasto. Unfortunately, I was a cookie dough kind of person.

The entrées ranged from burgers—Tofu Mushroom, Super Soy, Black Bean, and Turkey—to wraps such as the Five Mushroom, Hummus Leek, and Turkey Spinach. There were other dishes such as the Tofu Taco, Mushroom Pot Pie, Tuna Mushroom Melt, and Mushroom Ragout.

This explained why I never ate here.

The cost was amazingly affordable, most items under five dollars. I could see why the place was so popular to healthy eaters.

There was a lot of money to be made here.

And a lot to be stolen . . .

Behind Riley there was a pass-through to the kitchen, where I could only see hands working quickly and lettuce flying. No sign of Bill.

Down a long hall in front of me, just beyond the restrooms, a door was marked EMPLOYEES ONLY. I assumed Bill's office was back there . . .

I looked up as someone came out of the swinging door at the end of the hall, pushing a mop bucket. As she came closer I realized I recognized her.

"Noreen?"

Dark circles hovered under her Sally Jesse glasses. Her eyes narrowed while she apparently searched to put my name to my face, then widened in recognition.

"I didn't know you worked here," I said, inanely. How would I know?

A small gold tag on her black shirt read NOREEN, MANAGER. "Nepotism at its best," she said with no inflection at all.

Ahh. I remembered what Bill had said when I'd first met Noreen. *What are you doing here? Aren't you supposed to be at wo—*

Work.

That's how Bill had known Noreen.

She looked me up and down. "Not eating?"

"Picking up my son." Technically he wasn't mine, but I couldn't quite get my heart to accept that. "Riley."

"Oh, Bill's nephew." There was a look on her face I couldn't quite place.

I smiled. "Nepotism at its best."

I thought I saw the corner of her mouth lift into a small smile, but it could have been my imagination.

"Good kid," she said.

"Thanks. How's Greta holding up?" Maybe this was my way into seeing her. Noreen seemed to be the reasonable sort. And if she could get me in with Greta, I silently promised not to call her Mrs. Potato Head anymore. I'd even make it a commandment and everything.

"Still refuses to see anyone." Blunt cut bangs swung as she shook her head. "Shouldn't be alone at a time like this. It ain't right."

"Grief does funny things to people."

"She should be celebrating." She twirled the mop in the bucket. She must have seen my startled look. "No, I'm not sad he's gone. None of us here are. Especially Bill."

I perked up. "Oh?"

"He and Russ have differing management styles. There was constant staff turnover on the days Russ managed. Everyone loves working for Bill."

"Including you?"

She shrugged. "Better than Russ. Made me manager. Can't argue with that. After a year of working for Russ, I was still on the registers."

It seemed to me that pushing a mop around wasn't a step up from the registers.

"What made Russ want to start a restaurant? He was a little old for a middle-age crisis, wasn't he?"

Water sloshed out of the bucket. The scent of sautéed onions wafted through the pass-through, making my stomach growl despite itself.

Growl.

Ah. I finally understood the name. Sometimes I'm a little slow on the uptake.

Noreen pursed her lips. "Russ's always been a health nut. When that McDonald's documentary came out he'd finally had enough. He wanted to open a restaurant here in Freedom where people could have healthy options."

"Did Greta have a say?"

"Greta rarely had a say."

I thought about how sad that was, then said, "Why go in with Bill?"

She shot me a look that said she didn't know why she was talking to me, or telling me so much. I didn't quite understand it myself, but gift horses and all.

I swore under my breath.

"Something wrong?"

"My mother."

"Something's wrong with your mother?"

"No, no," I reassured. "Only that I'm the only one who got the defective cliché gene."

One dark bushy eyebrow arched over a squinty eye. I had the uneasy feeling she was trying to determine whether I was crazy.

If she figured it out, I wished she'd let me know.

The bucket got another glance from behind the Sally Jesse glasses, then she looked up at me again and picked up where we'd left off. "Bill had the know-how."

Apparently I rated over mopping. Good to know.

"Right. He'd managed previous places."

Noreen nodded, sloshed more water over the side of the bucket. At this rate the place would be flooded soon. "They both put in some money, Russ more than Bill. He was a miser, that Russ. Saved every penny."

"Well, it seems to have paid off. This place is doing well."

"Thanks to Bill. Without him, the place would have folded by now. Don't think Russ didn't know it. Originally he'd had plans to cut Bill loose after a year, but realized he couldn't run the place without him. Bill threatened to walk unless he was allowed to become a full co-owner. It's been tense around here ever since. With Russ wanting the place to himself and Bill thinking he deserves it all."

That wasn't quite the flowery version Lindsey had told me. Again I thought of my suspicions about Bill skimming from the business and pressed my luck. "Do you know why Russ brought Growl's accounting books home? Was he suspicious?"

"Suspicious of what?" Noreen asked. "The business is fine."

"That's right, it is," a male voice said.

It was Bill, and clearly he'd been eavesdropping. "The floor isn't going to mop itself, Noreen."

She looked like she wanted to give Bill a piece of her mind, but thought better of it. The wheels on the bucket squeaked as she pushed it toward the rear of the dining area. She didn't look back.

"Just picking up Riley," I said by way of explanation.

"He'll be out in a minute. Why are you so curious about the accounting books, Nina?"

"Curious? Me?" I laughed, desperately looked around for Riley.

"You've heard about curiosity and the cat, right?"

"Have you been hanging out with my mother?"

Flustered, he crossed his arms, unfolded them again. "What? Your mother? No, why?"

"Hey." Riley dropped a duffel bag at my feet. He'd changed from his black uniform to shorts and a tee. "I'm ready."

"Riley! Good to see you," I said, throwing an arm around him.

He shrugged out of the semihug, looked at me like I was crazy.

Scary. I was actually becoming accustomed to seeing that look from people.

"Gotta go." I fairly pushed Riley toward the door.

"What's with you?" he asked.

You've heard about curiosity and the cat, right?

Sounded suspiciously like a threat to me. What exactly could those accounting books reveal?

And how far would Bill go to conceal it?

Which was all too much to spill on Riley, so I opted for something he could relate to. "I have a date."

"With Bo-bby?" he singsonged.

"Dude," someone called just as I pushed open the door.

Riley turned and greeted the kid. "Hey, Goosh." The pair completed a series of hand slaps that left me dizzy.

"Goosh?" I said. He was tall, thin. The black Growl uniform hung loosely from his arms, his legs. Pockmarks scarred his face and a scraggly goatee hid his chin.

Long stringy hair covered Goosh's eyes. "It's, like, ah, whattaya call it? A um, yeah, nickname."

Thank God.

As he asked Riley, in a babbling almost incoherent string of words that would cause Mrs. Krauss to shudder, about covering for him the next day, I noticed how his words slurred. On closer inspection, his pupils were dark and wide.

My teeth set. The kid was clearly on something.

"Know him well?" I asked Riley as we climbed into my truck.

"We're not tight or anything."

I didn't know how to ask what I wanted to know.

"Don't worry." Riley chucked his duffel bag in the space behind the seats. "I'm not doing drugs."

I let out a breath of relief. "But Goosh is?"

Riley shrugged. "To each his own."

It sounded like something Kevin would say, and on the whole he was a pretty good dad. After all, he'd had the forethought to leave Riley with me when he'd moved in with Ginger Ho. Barlow. Ginger Barlow.

"Well, okay, then. Doesn't Bill mind, though? He has to notice."

"Can't do anything until Goosh fails a random drug test. So far he hasn't. Bill can get sued otherwise, since Goosh is actually pretty good at his job."

Sued. I shuddered. I never wanted to hear that word again.

I put the truck in reverse, then into drive. As we drove past Growl's door I couldn't help but notice Bill staring out at us.

Riley waved.

Me? I didn't wave. But the hair on the back of my neck stood up.

Sixteen

The Magic Sun Chinese Buffet had the best egg rolls ever. I was on my third.

"Not that hungry tonight?" Bobby asked.

"Ha. Ha."

Actually, I hadn't had much of an appetite until I walked in the door. The smells had done my stomach good. The hint of garlic, the soy sauce. Steamed vegetables.

It helped that with a full mouth I really couldn't talk.

I wished Bobby would eat more. He'd been rambling since we sat down about this and that. Nerves.

He was nervous.

About talking.

With me.

About something important.

I reached for another egg roll and took a sip of my water with lemon. The one strike against Magic Sun was that they didn't carry Dr Pepper. I forgave them because of the egg rolls.

Bobby pushed his plate aside. "Nina, we really need to talk."

Mouth full, I said, "We've been talking." Okay, he'd been talking. I'd been chewing.

He put his elbows on the table, leaned in. His dark blue eyes told me this was serious.

I'd known that, though, hadn't I?

I set my half-eaten egg roll down, pushed my plate aside too.

"All right." I put my elbows on the table in complete defiance of every one of my mother's manner lessons.

"I know you've been preoccupied lately, what with the death and all."

Great. I hadn't even been thinking of that. I'd been too wound up in what Bobby was going to say, do.

Now all I could see was Russ Grabinsky's stick figure outline in my head.

The egg rolls weren't sitting too well.

"Nina?"

"I'm fine."

"You sure?"

I nodded.

"Well, I have something I have to ask you. Something important. That I need you to think about. I know it's bad timing, but I need to know."

I braced myself. Was this really it? Was he asking me to marry him? Here? In the Magic Sun? If I said yes, would they put our picture over this little booth?

But I wasn't saying yes, was I? I couldn't. Not with Kevin, not with everything going on.

"Are you listening, Nina?"

I looked at Bobby. He was everything a girl could want. Everything. I wasn't blind. I saw his faults. Actually . . . I tried to think of a fault.

There had to be something.

"Nina?"

"Hmm?"

"Listening?"

I loved him. I did. It was a mixed-up sort of love, to be sure, because of all my confused feelings about Kevin, but it was love.

But marriage . . .

I couldn't.

It was too much, too soon.

Absolutely not.

No way.

"Nina?"

"Yes!" I shouted. The little Chinese woman tending the buffet dropped a pan of won-tons.

"Sorry," I said.

She hurriedly stuffed won-tons into the pan and looked at me as if I was possessed.

Bobby was smiling. "What?" I asked.

"Yes, what?"

"Yes, what? What?" Had I just agreed to marry him when he hadn't even asked?

He shook his head.

I reached for my egg roll.

I had been going to say yes.

Yes.

What was wrong with me?

"Listen."

I swallowed. "I'm listening."

"I've got a job offer. Principal of an elementary school."

"Bobby! That's great!" I leaned over, took his face in my hands and kissed him.

He didn't kiss back.

I sat back. "Not so great? Isn't being a principal what you've wanted?" I noticed there was paint under his short fingernails. White paint. Being a principal meant no more painting houses during the summer.

"It is."

"But?" My stomach started to hurt again.

"It's in Tampa."

"Tampa?"

"Florida."

"Oh."

"I know."

Kevin and I had once taken Riley to Disney World. It took us fourteen hours to drive there. Tampa had to be close to that.

Fourteen hours by car. Three by plane.

It would make dating tough.

I bit the inside of my cheek to stem the tingling in my nose, my eyes.

I would not cry.

This was something Bobby wanted.

Deserved.

"When do you leave?"

He reached across the table, took my hand. "That's just it, Nina."

"What is?"

"I guess that's up to you."

"Me? How?"

"There's only one thing keeping me here."

The tingling started again.

"And I need to know. Do I stay?" He squeezed my hand. "Or do I go?"

Tam was asleep by the time I made it to the hospital. I set Sassy, her African violet, on her bedside table, and I swear the thing looked perkier immediately.

There was evidence my mother had been there, namely the French chocolates and the custom balloon that read "Get well, *chérie*."

The curtain around Brickhouse's bed was pulled tight. It was just as well. I didn't want to see her right now.

On my way out of the Magic Sun, I'd grabbed a handful of fortune cookies. Not one of them told me what to do with Bobby, though I now had enough lottery numbers for the next month.

He'd kissed me good-bye, helped me into my car, and watched me drive away.

I'd told him I needed some time.

He hadn't looked surprised. Just sad.

Which broke my heart.

Should I stay or should I go?

It was a lot of pressure, and I decided after my fifth fortune cookie, that it wasn't a fair question. To lay that all on me. To let me decide his fate. What if I said stay and then things didn't work out between us? What if I said go and it was the worst mistake I'd ever made?

I sighed, patted Tam's tummy, and turned to go. I hesitated as I walked to the door, feeling slightly guilty that I hadn't even checked on Brickhouse.

Rolling my eyes at myself, I pulled back the curtain around the bed. No need for the guilt.

The bed was empty; Brickhouse was gone.

Monday morning. I popped open a sleep-filled eye, looked at the clock. Six-thirty.

Time to get up.

Instead I dragged my new down comforter over my head.

Monday mornings were supposed to be filled with promise. Of hope that the week ahead would be a good one.

Pipes rattled as Riley flushed the toilet.

I thought it a good harbinger of what *my* week ahead would be like.

Harbinger.

Heh. Mrs. Krauss would be proud.

I groaned, thinking of Brickhouse. I'd checked with the nurses' station—she'd been discharged. Which meant she was on the loose and could show up anywhere. Anytime.

I shuddered, dragged the covers off my head. *"Eeeee!"* I screamed when I saw a face looming over me.

"Sorry!" Riley said. "Didn't mean to scare you. Your door was open."

I'd taken to leaving it open since Kevin moved out. I didn't know why and didn't want to pay for the therapy that would tell me.

"Can you drive me to work?"

"This early?" I asked. "Growl doesn't open till eleven. What time are you due in?"

"Ten-thirty."

I blinked at the clock, wondering if I'd read it wrong the first time: 6:36.

Riley saw me looking. "Uncle Bill gave me a key to get in on the mornings I opened."

"A key to a fifteen-year-old?"

"Almost sixteen. And it's for his *nephew*. Jeez. Do you think I'm going to rob the place? I figure I'd just hang out until Bill gets there, maybe do some cleaning. Stocking. Whatever. I'd leave at ten except I can't skateboard yet," he said, holding up his still-splinted hand, "and Dad's at work . . ."

"I can drive you," I said, tossing covers. "But how about you come to TBS with me until ten?" I didn't want to mention that I was worried about him being alone at Growl until Bill showed up. "You can answer phones."

"Do I get paid?"

I growled. "Yes." I thought about what I paid Tam, then subtracted . . . a lot. "Six bucks an hour."

"What? That's barely minimum wage."

"Take it or leave it."

"Take it."

I smiled and headed for my bathroom before I realized I didn't have a bathroom. The demo crew was due at nine. My mother was due at eight. I needed to be out of there before then.

I grabbed my robe. "Did you leave me any hot water?"

"First come, first serve," he said, walking out the door.

Harbingers, indeed.

Seventeen

The chimes sang as I pulled open the TBS door, Riley right on my heels. I stopped short at the sight greeting me, and Riley barreled into me, knocking me to the floor.

Brickhouse clucked. "You're a clumsy one, aren't you?"

I looked up at Riley, who gave me an it-wasn't-my-fault shrug. He did offer me a hand up, though.

I'd take what I could get. "What are you doing here?" I asked Brickhouse.

"Working."

"Working?"

"Miss Tamara hired me. And by the looks of it, none too soon. This place has gone to heck in a handbasket."

Heck. In a handbasket.

I wanted to tell her where she could go in a handbasket.

It wasn't heck.

"Great," Riley said. "What am I going to do now?"

Mrs. Krauss clucked. "I can use a capable assistant, young man. I think you're just what I need. And my, don't you look snazzy?"

Snazzy. Hmmph. I didn't think that was a vocabulary word I ever learned in her English class.

"Uniform. I've got to work later."

"At Growl, right?"

"You've been there?"

"Ach, no. I cannot take such organic food. I get gas."

Way too much information.

"They have medicine for that, you know," Riley said.

I left the two of them to their conversation. It was just past eight. Unfortunately I'd given everyone the day off, so now I'd be alone with Brickhouse.

All day.

I wondered which one of us would survive it.

I wished Kit were coming in. Or Coby. Or Marty. Or anyone. I'd even take Harry von Barber at this point.

With a mini coming up on Wednesday, tomorrow would be filled with meetings, checklists, and confirmation phone calls.

As I sat at my desk, signed onto my server, I couldn't help but think again about cutting back. As it was right now, TBS usually worked two full makeovers and two to three minis a week. It was a lot of work. A lot of hours. Especially during the summer. I didn't want to get burned out. And I wanted my crew to have a life.

Should I stay or should I go?

And possibly me too.

I needed to sit down soon to crunch numbers. Decide which direction to take TBS.

I had meetings booked solid from one till four. At five I had to go meet with Derrick Brandt at his nursery. I had several orders placed, and I wanted to make sure he'd gotten all the materials I needed.

I tapped my pen on my ink-stained blotter and wondered how Tam was doing. Instead of just sitting there thinking about her, I picked up the phone and dialed the hospital. I punched in her room number. No one answered.

Could be she was in the bathroom. Or having tests done.

But I doubted it. She'd sent Brickhouse to work for me.

Knowing how I felt about her.

Tam would be avoiding me like the—

I stopped myself in the nick of time.

Brickhouse's laughter carried through my closed door, grated my nerves.

It was a good thing Tam wasn't around.

I spent some time going through my e-mails, writing some checks. A large one to Stanley Mack. It hurt to write it, but he was worth every cent. His invoice for the Grabinsky job was probably in the mail.

The Lockharts had thankfully paid me up front, in full. But that didn't change the fact that the job hadn't been done yet.

I buzzed Brickhouse through the intercom. "Have there been any messages from Greta Grabinsky?"

"Oh, the woman suing you?"

"You're getting sued?" Riley asked, his voice an octave higher than normal.

Brickhouse clucked. "You didn't know?"

Riley clucked too. God, it was contagious. "No!"

"Hello!" I said. "Messages?"

"You really should share your troubles with your family."

Great. Now a lecture.

"Yeah," Riley piped in.

My jaw clenched. If Brickhouse continued working for me I was going to need to get one of those retainers people wear for TMJ. "Messages?"

"No."

I stabbed the intercom button.

I wondered if Russ's autopsy had been done yet. It was horrible that I hoped the M.E. would find something. Anything that would exonerate me.

There were plenty of people who hated the man, wanted him dead.

Whoever Russ was blackmailing, for one.

Bill was high on that list too.

His employees hated him.

Noreen hated him.

Even Greta had motive if it was true about her horrible marriage.

Yet the prosecutor wanted to file charges against me.

Ridiculous.

I reached in my bottom drawer for a notepad and my breath caught at the sight of the Almond Joys.

The Almond Joys Bobby sent me weekly.

So far I'd done a good job not thinking about him, his job offer, even though I knew I had to at some point soon.

The phone rang, but I let Brickhouse answer. It was apparently what I was paying her for.

A second later her annoying voice came through the speaker on my desk. "Detective Quinn, line one."

"Thanks. I'll take it. Hey," I said, picking up the phone.

"Hey you. How you holding up?"

"Fine." Why was Kevin calling? Had he heard something? "Any word on the murder charges?"

I heard a gasp and yelled, "Hang up, Mrs. Krauss!"

One loud cluck and phone click later, I picked up the conversation.

"Brickhouse is working for you?" Kevin asked.

"Are you laughing? Because it's not funny."

"Is so."

"Tam hired her."

"Then she's staying."

"Pretty much."

"Good thing Tam's safe in the hospital."

"Pretty much."

Because I had to make a decision about Bobby, I asked, "How's Parsley?"

I'd caught him off guard. The silence on his end of the line was telling. "Fine."

It was also telling that he didn't correct Ginger's name, his usual habit. "You two still getting along?"

"You know how I feel about you, Nina. I made that clear already."

A while back he'd asked me, hypothetically, what would happen between us if he realized he'd made a big mistake in leaving.

Even though I still loved him, I hadn't been able to forgive him.

"And it didn't change things," he said, "so what's changed?"

I needed to decide about Bobby, that's what. Which meant that I needed to decide, once and for all, about Kevin.

Were we done? For good? Was I just hanging on to broken hopes and crushed dreams?

I wasn't sure. And I wasn't sure how to be sure.

Lord, I was beginning to suspect I needed motherly advice.

My confusion was that bad.

"Nina?"

"It's nothing."

"Sounds like something to me."

"Too much time at the range. Your hearing's going."

He grunted. "Stubborn."

"Why'd you call?"

"Russ Grabinsky."

"You have heard something, then."

"I haven't heard about the charges, but the M.E. just faxed over the postmortem results."

"And?"

"And they're still waiting for the tox screens to come back, so it's not a final report."

"But?"

He didn't lower his voice, so I assumed he was on his cell somewhere, safe from prying ears. "Heart attack. Ninety-five percent artery blockage. He was a walking time bomb."

"A time bomb. One that could be set off by a surprise makeover?"

"I'm sorry."

"So the prosecutor will probably file charges against me."

"I don't know. Nothing will happen until the toxicology reports come in. There could be something in there."

Could be. But probably not.

I sighed. "Thanks for letting me know. I know you're not supposed to be talking to me."

"I'll always do my best to protect you, Nina. You've got to know that."

Funny thing was I did.

After dropping Riley off at Growl, I drove over to the Fallow Falls neighborhood.

I pulled right into Greta's driveway, marched up the front steps, and rang the bell.

Coming here served two purposes. One was to avoid contact with Brickhouse Krauss at all costs. The other was to talk with Greta Grabinsky.

I wasn't leaving until I saw her. That was that. I had too much to lose if I didn't. She could sue the pants off me if she wanted, but I was not going to jail for something that wasn't my fault.

I rang the bell again.

Greta held a lot of the answers I wanted. About Bill and Russ, those accounting books, the HOA lawsuit, the person threatening her, about finishing the backyard.

Buzzing again, I tapped my foot. The pot of pansies on the front step looked pitiful, wilting in the sunshine.

Giving up on the buzzer, I rapped on the door. It opened on its own.

Immediately my defenses went up.

"Hello?" I called, pushing the door farther open with my elbow. "Mrs. Grabinsky? Greta?"

Don't go in, my inner voice whispered.

The adrenaline drowned it out.

I stepped into a small hallway. The lime green linoleum was worn and cracked but looked freshly cleaned. I came to two doorways, one on each side of me. I went left. The living room.

I gasped. Where the room had been immaculate the other day, it was now as though a twister had swept through, up-ending and damaging everything in its path.

My gaze immediately shot to the small end table where just two days ago the accounting books had sat. The over-turned table lay on its side.

I poked around as best I could without touching anything, but as far as I could tell, the accounting books were gone.

The sofa's cushions had been slashed open, stuffing spilling out of the wounds. The couch itself had been tipped, its underside ripped open.

Someone had been looking for something.

The voice from the other day, the one coming from Greta's kitchen, haunted me.

If he had them, you had them. And I want them back. Now. Russ had no right to them and neither do you.

Had he finally given up on Greta giving the item back and resorted to taking it back? By force?

"Greta?" I called out.

I took another minute to look around the living room, at the broken face of the old grandfather clock, the old typewriter upside down on the floor, the old buffet cabinet turned on its side, its doors open wide.

The dining room hadn't fared much better. Whoever had been searching was careful not to break any of the good china.

How courteous.

A set of silver littered the floor. Nothing looked missing, though I supposed Greta would have to be the one to go through things piece by piece.

I felt myself getting angry for her. This kind of intrusion was such a violation of privacy and security.

"Greta?" I yelled.

Get out, my inner voice yelled.

I listened, but only for a second. I couldn't leave until I knew if Greta was okay.

In the kitchen, the cabinets and pantry had been emptied onto the floor. The searcher was thorough. Even the flour and sugar canisters were dumped out—into the sink.

Trash spilled out of a plastic white can onto the linoleum. A brown banana peel, old newspaper, a take-out soup cup from Growl that still had mushrooms clinging to its insulated sides. Forest Mushroom? Mushroom Barley? There was also a Growl take-out bag, coffee grounds, and some wadded paper towels.

I quickly checked the back hall. More of the same destruction. But no Greta.

A brown rotary phone hung on the kitchen wall, and I told myself to call the police.

I headed for the stairs instead.

On the second floor the bathroom was a mess, drawers opened. I tried not to notice the everyday items of Russ and Greta's life. The toothpaste, the deodorant, razors, shaving cream, but couldn't. It smelled horrid in there even though the window was open. The scent of someone who'd been horribly ill. Lingering from Russ's bout with the flu?

The window looked out into the backyard, and from up there was a bird's-eye view of both the Lockharts' and the Hathaways' yards. I took a deep breath of clean air and hurried into the hall.

There were only two bedrooms. I went for the closest and pushed open the door. "Greta? Are you here?"

The first thing I noticed was that this room hadn't been searched.

The second was that Greta lay diagonally across the bed on her back, wearing the same frumpy housecoat she'd worn the last two times I'd seen her.

Only this time she was very clearly dead.

Eighteen

I'd been told not to go anywhere by the baby-faced officer first on the scene. Not that I could—his car blocked the end of the driveway.

Brickhouse had clucked when I called to cancel my one o'clock appointment. I hadn't told her why.

Officer Baby Face had informed me detectives would want to speak with me, and my stomach hurt really bad, so I had a good idea just who those detectives would be.

I sat on my front bumper and looked at the house. Russ had died of a heart attack. What had killed Greta?

I hadn't seen anything that would indicate she'd been murdered. No blood, no bruising. But it just seemed too coincidental that she'd die of natural causes during a burglary.

Who'd broken in?

I tilted my head, looked at the Lockharts' house. The accounting books were the only things I could say for certain were missing. And Bill had been looking for them.

I jumped to the conclusion and figured he'd taken them.

But why ransack the rest of the house? To make it look like someone else had done it?

The man from Greta's kitchen? That person would make a

great scapegoat. How convenient that Bill had heard the man's threats.

And Greta? Had she gotten in the way?

I looked up. Uh-oh.

"You," Kevin said, approaching me. "Come with us."

"Us" included Ginger. My day just kept getting better and better.

Officers had begun roping off the house with crime scene tape. Kevin led me back to his car, an unmarked black Crown Vic with a long antenna on its trunk.

Ginger followed. She was tall, with long legs that reminded me of the spider in my window. Her hair was tied back in a long ponytail. She had beautiful wide eyes, full lips, a kind, caring face. If I were being truthful, she was gorgeous.

I hated that about her.

I sat there through thirty minutes of Kevin and Ginger's repetitive questions, trying not to compare myself to her. I told them over and over what I knew, what I saw. I even reminded them about Greta's visitor the other day. And I even told them about the missing account books.

That's me. Nina Colette Good Citizen Ceceri Quinn.

While I was at it, I shared my theory about why the Lockharts had hired me—to induce a heart attack on purpose.

Kevin didn't say anything at that, just arched an eyebrow.

Hmmph.

"Anything else?" he finally said.

"I told Riley I'd pick him up tonight, so you don't have to."

"He called."

Ginger wandered off.

Kevin looked over his shoulder, watched her go, then turned back to me. "What's with that call this morning?"

"You called me."

He stepped in. He smelled good. "You know what I mean."

"Nope."

"Nina . . ."

"Kevin."

"Are you having second thoughts?"

And thirds and fourths. I played dumb. "About what?"

"About us."

His sparkly green eyes lingered on my lips. It felt like the temperature had gone up a few degrees. I was suddenly sweating, and suddenly worried my deodorant wasn't strong enough, thanks to what Kit had said yesterday.

"Us?"

"Yes, us."

The divorce would be final in seven days. I put my hand on my stomach, but it didn't help the pain.

"You okay?"

"Fine." Maybe I'd call the doctor when I got back, see if she'd fit me in.

"When'd you last eat?"

I thought about it, figured it was those egg rolls last night. No wonder my stomach hurt. "I'm okay. Really."

With his finger, he lifted my chin. "I don't like what's going on here," he said.

"With us?"

He smiled. "I knew there was more to that call this morning."

I scowled.

"I actually meant with the Grabinskys. You be careful. Don't get any ideas about snooping. I know how you are."

"Yes, sir." My fingers were crossed behind my back.

As soon as he turned, I looked around for Kate Hathaway, found her at the edge of the gathering crowd. I just wanted to ask her a few questions before I left.

I was glad to see that she was alone, that Meredith wasn't lurking around anywhere.

"This is horrible," Kate said when she spotted me. "Who would do such a thing?"

"It could have been natural. You're always hearing about stories of people who've been married forever dying days apart. Of broken hearts."

"With a ransacked house?"

She had a point. Still, I hadn't seen any signs of a struggle inside Greta's room. And nothing on her body that suggested she'd been killed.

Actually, I'd been thinking about it, and it seemed more likely with those bathroom odors that she had gotten the flu going around and maybe died from that.

After all, Russ had had it. It would seem likely Greta would get it too. Maybe she had other health issues that made it too hard to fight the bug. I wished I had snooped through the medicine cabinet when I'd had the chance.

"Do the police think this was a random break-in? One of those home invasions?"

I could see her presidential wheels spinning. If there were a burglar in the neighborhood . . .

"I don't know." I had my doubts about the randomness of it all but kept them to myself, per Kevin's strict orders.

I heard a car door slam and saw Dale Hathaway striding across his driveway toward his wife. She must have called him away from work.

My phone rang. Tam. I stepped aside to answer it.

"Did you kill someone else?"

I dropped my voice. "I didn't kill anyone!"

"I heard there was another dead body."

Dear Lord. "How'd you hear that?"

"Lindsey Lockhart called Bill at Growl. Riley heard about it and called you at work, but got Ursula, and Ursula called me."

My mind spun trying to keep up with it.

"Well," I said, "do you know if Bill was coming home?" I really wanted to ask him about those accounting books.

"Riley said something about him leaving early."

"Wait, you talked to Riley?"

"I needed more information, Nina. This hospital room isn't exactly control room central."

"How are you feeling?"

"Better. The doctor says I might be able to go home soon."

"Really?"

"I'll still be on bed rest, though. How's Ursula working out by the way? Isn't she perfect for the job?"

Depended on what job. Driving me crazy, definitely. I wasn't sold on the receptionist part. Not yet at least. "She's doing better than Coby." Which was true.

"I knew you'd be happy to have her."

"Tam, get your head checked while you're at the hospital."

"Now, Nina, I know you two aren't the best of friends, but she's really a nice—"

"Gotta go," I said before I threw up. " 'Bye!"

I snapped my phone closed, wandered back to Kate and Dale.

Suddenly I was hearing Disney's chipmunk song in my head. I definitely needed food.

My phone rang again. I sighed, stepped away and answered it, wondering if Tam had figured out what was going on from her hospital bed and was calling to let me know.

"Chérie?"

"Mom? What's wrong?"

"Wrong? Wrong? Nothing's wrong. What makes you say that?"

"The tone of your voice."

"Tone? What tone?"

"Mom."

"There's been a small problem here. Very small. I'm sure the insurance will cover it."

I closed my eyes, tried to rub both throbbing temples with one hand. "What kind of problem?"

"A broken pipe is all. Nothing major."

A broken pipe. On the second floor.

"Just thought I'd let you know. I'll let you get back to work now. Ta!"

"Trouble?" Kate asked when she saw my face.

I wanted to laugh. Could this day get any worse?

"Nothing the insurance can't cover, apparently."

"Oh."

Cops streamed from the Grabinsky doorway. Across the yard, I saw Meredith Adams staring at me. I wanted to stick my tongue out. I restrained.

"This is all so sad," Dale said. He held Kate protectively, his arm wrapped around her shoulder. The sun glinted off his wedding ring.

A ring I'd seen before.

In Greta's kitchen.

Close up I could see the unusual design more clearly than I had the other day.

Platinum twigs intertwined to form a beautiful floating band. Kate, I suddenly noticed, had a matching one.

"We love to hike. We love nature of all kinds," Kate said.

I must have looked confused.

"The wedding rings. I saw you looking at Dale's."

"They're beautiful." I looked up at Dale.

"Custom made," he said. "Nothing but the best for Kate."

Russ had been blackmailing Dale.

Dale had threatened Greta.

I looked at Kate. Did she know?

I wondered what it was Russ had on Dale. He looked

like a loving husband, but I knew looks could be deceiving.

Had it been Dale who trashed the Grabinsky house?

Had Greta been murdered after all? What had Dale said to Greta? Something about her paying dearly?

"I'm going to go," I said.

They went back to their house too. I managed to find Baby Face and had him move his patrol car. Before I left, I grabbed a bottle of spring water from my truck, crossed the police line, and poured it into the pot of pansies on the porch. I didn't want another thing to die at this house.

I backed out of the driveway and started driving, realizing I was shaking.

It had been one of those days. I needed some food, some Advil, some comfort, a hug.

It wasn't until I was almost there that I realized where I was going.

Bobby.

Nineteen

By four-fifteen I was in a seriously bad mood.

Bobby wasn't to be found, the Advil hadn't worked, nothing looked or sounded good enough to eat, and there was no one around to hug.

Well, there was Brickhouse, but I had my limits.

Too bad Kit wasn't there. The man gave the best hugs ever.

I looked around my office. Two design boards leaned against my desk, which was cluttered with site plans and designs.

To add insult to my day, when I'd visited Derrick Brandt at the nursery, I learned that Jean-Claude hadn't placed the orders I needed. Luckily, with what Derrick had in stock, we were able to salvage my design plans.

I'd come back to the office for my appointments and learned that my two o'clock had bailed on me after hearing the news reports of Russ's death.

Thankfully, the young couple who came in at three was very enthusiastic and excited about doing a yard for the young woman's mother.

I double-checked that I had the written permission of at least one homeowner (the girl's father) before I took them on.

Jean-Claude, Jean Claude.

I rubbed my temples. What was I going to do?

Grabbing my cell phone, I punched in Ana's number, waited while it rang.

"Ana Bertoli," she chirped.

"You sound happy."

"Shakes and I are talking."

"Shakes?"

"S. Larue's nickname. I can live with Shakes. It's kind of cute."

"Talking? Are you back together?"

"Not yet, but we're working on it. You sound like crap," she said. "What's wrong?"

She knew me too well to hide anything. "Too long to get into."

"Want me to come over tonight?"

If she and S. Larue were talking, I thought that maybe she'd have other plans. "I'm okay."

"You sure?"

"Yep. Hey, did you ever hear from that bartender?"

"Jake? He was cute, wasn't he?"

"Shakes," I reminded.

"I can look."

"No you can't. You're easily distracted."

"I take exception to that."

"No you don't."

"You're right. Nope, haven't heard from Jake. Why? Has JC disappeared again?"

"Ugh. Don't call him that."

"Why? It's . . . cute."

"You're in a cute mood."

"Love is in the air."

I wanted to gag.

"Are you gagging?"

"I'm close."

"Why? You've got Bo-bby."

Why did everyone singsong his name? "He might be leaving."

"What? Spill!"

I explained about the transfer.

"Stop thinking about how Kevin would feel."

Leave it to Ana to cut to the heart of the matter.

"It's not up to him. It's your life, Nina."

"I know."

"Do you?"

"Kind of." Argh.

"I'll be over at eight."

"No, no. I'm fine."

"I'll bring Phish Food."

"All right." I'm easily swayed by Ben & Jerry's.

"Besides, I want to see your bedroom. I hear it's gorgeous."

"It is. But the bathroom . . ."

"Bathroom?"

"You don't want to know."

We hung up, and I was clearing clutter (stuffing things in drawers) when Brickhouse appeared in my doorway.

She clucked.

I closed my eyes, thought about thunking my head on my desk until I was unconscious. I didn't have the energy for Brickhouse right now.

When I opened my eyes, she was right in front of my desk, a bowl in her hands. She set it in front of me.

"Eat."

I peeked into the bowl. The smell that rose up on waves of steam made my stomach growl.

There were things in there I couldn't identify. Little bits of pudgy rice-shaped pasta for one. The spices for another. I recognized the carrots, the celery, the bits of ground beef. "What is it?"

"Soup."

"Ha. Ha."

"It's an old family recipe." She set a plastic spoon next to the bowl. "Now eat."

I looked up, trying to gauge why she was being nice to me, and thought I saw a flash of maternal worry before her eyes switched back to their normal blue steel.

"Thanks," I said, nearly choking on the word. Me, thanking Brickhouse Krauss. I never thought I'd see the day.

She nodded and walked out the door.

I scooped, I sipped, I *mmmm*ed. It was very, very good.

I just hoped it wasn't poisoned.

Inside Growl, people stood four deep in lines. There were three people working the registers. Two looked like they could have been Goosh's brother and sister.

I stood there twirling my key chain on my finger until Riley noticed me. He gave me the one-finger wait-a-minute sign again. I pointed down the hallway that led to the restrooms.

He nodded.

I didn't see Noreen, and according to Tam, Bill had gone home early. This was the perfect time to check his office, see if those accounting books had miraculously turned up.

Black ceramic tile led me to the ladies' room. I stopped, looked over my shoulder, and sprinted down the rest of the hallway toward the Employees Only door, Keds squeaking, keys jangling.

Pushing on the swinging door, I peeked in. Didn't see anyone. Slipping through the opening, I looked around.

To my right, a short hallway led to the kitchen area and what looked like a break room. Someone stood with their back to me, chopping tomatoes.

There was an office to the left, the light off, the door open. I ducked in, closed the door, turned on the light.

The office was split down the middle by a partition. Each half matched the other, right down to the heavy oak desk and steel trash can. Two small supply closets faced each other on opposite walls.

One desk had a picture of Lindsey on it. Bill's. My Clue-playing abilities never ceased to amaze me. Setting my keys on the heavy duty industrial carpet, I riffled through papers, opened drawers. No accounting books. Nothing that looked the least bit incriminating at all.

Working fast, I checked Russ's desk as well. The man was a neatnik, I'd give him that. Tam would have appreciated his organizing. I looked for a financial file among the hanging files but couldn't find one.

Bracing myself, I opened the closet door on Russ's side, hoping nothing—namely a dead body—fell out on me.

It had been that kind of day.

There were several work shirts hanging on a rod, and shelves above and below that held office supplies. Printer paper, file folders, envelopes, and the like.

Quickly, I crossed the room to Bill's closet, turned the handle.

It was locked.

Why? What was in there?

My mind jumped again to dead bodies.

Pushing that thought away, I wished I'd brought my purse in. My credit card would have come in handy right about now. Kevin had once shown me how incredibly easy it was to bypass a simple lock.

And this one was simple.

I didn't bother checking my hair for a bobby pin—I never used them. I thought fast.

The desk. It would have paper clips. Sure enough, they were in the top drawer. An economy-size box of them. I grabbed one, unbent it.

A second later the lock released.

Slowly, I opened the door.

"Ewww." I stepped back.

Not a dead body, but almost as bad.

Mushrooms.

I shuddered.

Two small barrels of them took up two-thirds of the closet floor. There was an empty space on the left side that looked just the right size for another barrel. Shelves started above the barrels, right about thigh high, and went all the way to the ceiling. They were filled with everything from humongous jars of fat-free mayonnaise (ewww) to cans of chick peas, black beans, barley, and lentils (double ewww).

It was a storage closet.

Not an accounting book to be found. And I looked. Behind cans of mandarin oranges, bags of rice, spice tins. Despite myself, I even poked around the mushroom barrels.

If Bill had taken the accounting books from Greta's house, he hadn't brought them here. Not that I could find them anyway. Maybe he'd kept them at home? Less suspicion that way.

The office doorknob jiggled. My stomach lurched.

"Why is this door locked?"

Bill. Oh God.

"I don't know."

Noreen.

I looked around for a place to hide. My gaze hit on the closet floor. I might be able to make it . . . if I squeezed.

Hard.

"How odd," Bill said. Muffled, his voice sounded menacing.

I ran over to the light switch, flipped it as I heard a key sliding into the lock. I fairly dove into the closet, became a contortionist, and closed the door behind me.

It was dark. Very dark.

And oddly chilly.

And smelly.

For a second I had a panic attack about my deodorant again, then realized the smell wasn't coming from me. It was the mushrooms.

I shuddered again. Mushrooms and I just didn't get along. Not since my mother made beef Stroganoff when I was six and forced me to eat every revolting bite. It probably had more to do with my mother's cooking than the mushrooms themselves, but it had scarred me, and my stomach, for life.

I didn't know a lot about mushrooms—just that I didn't like them—but weren't they supposed to be stored in a refrigerator?

Or a cool, dry place like a storage closet? my inner voice asked.

I told it to be quiet, because I should have realized that myself. I really hated being wrong.

The office door swung open, its hinges in need of WD-40. I held my breath, afraid Bill and Noreen could somehow hear me breathing. Despite the coolness, sweat trickled down the side of my head, tickling my ear. I rubbed it on my shoulder.

I heard a click, and light suddenly filtered through the cracks in the closet door as the overhead fluorescents in the office clicked and popped, giving me just enough hazy illumination to make out shapes.

When I started to see spots, I finally took a deep breath, but was suddenly overcome by the same claustrophobic feeling I experience when I scuba dive. I gave up holding my breath and opted for closing my eyes. I practiced Lamaze breathing again.

When it came time for me to have a baby, I'd be all set.

Babies. Bobby.

I gave myself a mental shake. This wasn't the time!

Leaning my head against the closet wall, I wished I hadn't given up on gymnastics when I was a kid. Flexibility and I didn't get along. My knees screamed, my back ached, and something dug into my back. A bracket for the shelves. My thighs tingled—the beginning of a Charlie horse.

I tried to flex my foot and nearly kicked the basket of mushrooms. I stayed put. What was a little pain?

I could handle it.

"Has anyone else been in here?" Bill's voice was so clear, so loud, he had to have been standing on the other side of the door.

"Not that I know of." Noreen's voice sounded strained, stiff.

What was she doing here? She must have been notified by the police that Greta had died. Wouldn't she be at the house? At the hospital where they'd taken the body for an autopsy?

Not that she could do much at either place.

"I, um, might have locked it."

Riley? I stiffened, and regretted it immediately.

I bit my lip against the pain of the Charlie horse and kneaded my thigh, trying to get rid of it, all the while wondering what Riley was doing with Bill and Noreen. Wasn't he working the register? How long had I been in the office?

Holding my watch up to a sliver of light, I realized I'd been snooping for fifteen minutes.

"When I came in to get, uh, some cash register tape earlier. My mom always makes me lock up when I leave the house. Habit. Sorry."

"It's okay," Bill said.

My mind raced. Had Riley just called me his mom? Had I been hearing things? Had I been sniffing too many fungus fumes?

His mom.

Tears gathered in my eyes, and I looked up, trying to keep

them in. Something taped to the underside of the bottom shelf near the mushroom barrels caught my eye. I squinted, trying to make it out.

I didn't dare move, but from where I was it looked like a manila envelope.

"What're you doing down there?" Bill asked.

"Tying my shoe," Riley answered. "Not so easy with this splint."

"Need help?" Noreen asked.

"Nope. Got it. Thanks."

"You need a ride home?" Bill asked.

"No, my mom's coming," Riley said.

There it was again. Mom.

My heart produced a weird warm and fuzzy feeling, and I basked in it for a second before I stiffened again.

I barely held in the *Owww* as my thigh spasmed. Tears did come, but it was from the pain, not any kind of lovey-dovey maternal feelings.

The spasm eased, the pain lessened, and I remembered why I had stiffened in the first place.

Riley. Lying. Not just about me not being there yet to pick him up, but about locking the door in the first place.

Why?

Did he somehow know I was in here?

How?

As quietly as I could, I felt my pockets.

No keys.

They were sitting on the floor next to Bill's desk!

Right near where Riley had "tied his shoes"? I hoped so.

"I think I'll just go get something to eat while I wait for her."

Ewww. Eat something? From here? Had I taught that boy nothing?

"You need to call her?" Bill asked.

"No, she's usually late. I'm used to it."

Hmmph.

Footsteps faded.

"Get some rest, Noreen. Take as much time off as you need."

Maybe Bill wasn't such a bad guy after all.

"I'm just going to grab my purse and go. I ran out of here so fast this afternoon, I forgot it."

"I'm really sorry about Greta."

"Me too." Noreen's voice cracked, and I felt my throat tighten with sympathy.

I heard some rustling of clothes and imagined Bill giving Noreen a hug.

"Call when you're ready to come back. I'll put you on the schedule."

"All right."

I heard papers shuffling, then a cell phone ringing. I panicked until I realized it wasn't mine. Mine was in my backpack, and that was in the truck.

"Lockhart . . . Yeah, tonight's fine. My supply is really low." He laughed. "Yes, business is good, especially now that Russ is out of the picture."

There went my opinion of Bill, once and for all. Okay, so it wasn't an admission that he'd had something to do with Russ's death, but it was clear enough he'd wanted Russ gone.

Enough to formulate an elaborate plan to give the man a heart attack?

I listened to Bill make arrangements for something to be delivered that night. I thought I heard him leave the room, but couldn't be sure.

How would I be sure? I couldn't see through the cracks in the door frame. I certainly wasn't Superman. Woman. Whatever.

I decided to stay hidden until I hadn't heard Bill for ten minutes.

My thigh throbbed and I desperately wanted to move, to readjust. Then my eye caught that envelope again.

I wiggled slowly, trying not to make a sound, and reached for the envelope. It took some doing, some praying, and lots of patience, but I finally freed it.

A metal clasp bit into my finger as I lifted the flap. Inside were two business-size envelopes. I pulled them out, held them each up to the streak of light.

Each said the same thing in a strange typed font. "Bill Lockhart. Personal."

My eyebrow went up. Interesting.

There was no way I could read the letters without making a ruckus, so I did the next best thing.

Stole them.

Really, I had to talk with Father Keesler soon.

It took more patience than I thought I had, but I finally got the manila envelope back where it had come from, and stuffed the two other envelopes down my shirt, which was thankfully tucked in.

After exactly ten minutes by my trusty Timex, I pressed my ear to the door to listen for noise just as it swung open. I fell out in a ball onto someone's feet, my limbs not realizing they were free.

I looked up into accusing eyes.

Twenty

"You can stop saying sorry," Riley said, climbing into my TBS truck, "and start telling me why you were in Bill's office in the first place."

"When does driver's ed end? Maybe we can look at some used cars." I held out my hand for my keys. Sure enough, Riley had them. He dropped them into my palm.

"Don't try to distract me," he said. "What were you doing in Bill's closet?"

This was surreal. Grilling *from* a teenager.

"Research," I said. "On mushrooms."

He stared.

He did it well.

I cracked. "I was looking for something."

"What kind of something? Does this have to do with Ebenezer's death?"

Did it?

"I don't know."

I started the engine, turned toward home.

"I bet Dad would want to know what you were doing in that closet."

I shot him a *you wouldn't* look.

He gave me an *oh yes I would.*

"Go ahead and tell him."

That took him by surprise. Little did he know I had a greater fear of being blackmailed by him than facing Kevin.

Mom.

I wondered now if he'd said it as a ploy. That he knew I'd been in the closet and it was his way of telling me he knew I was in there.

Because it was just so out of character.

And . . . familial.

As I turned toward home, I decided not to ask. Too desperate.

"Well, did you find it?"

"No."

But I'd found something else. Those letters. I hoped they were worth the pain. My legs were still cramping.

"Why'd it take you so long to come get me?" I asked.

"I figured you'd come out when Bill left."

"I didn't know for certain if Bill had left! One minute he's on the phone making plans for a delivery tonight, and the next thing I know it's quiet. Is he doing paperwork? Napping? I couldn't just come out."

"A delivery tonight?"

"That's what I heard. Why?"

"We only get deliveries in the morning. That's strange."

That was strange.

These last few days had been strange.

"Maybe mushrooms?" I said. "It looked like there was a barrel missing from that closet."

There was an odd look on Riley's face. "Maybe."

"What maybe? Do you know something?"

"Maybe."

"Riley Michael."

"Nina Colette."

I growled.

He glared.

This was getting us nowhere.

"You tell me what you were doing in that closet, and I'll tell you what I think I might know."

I said, "This isn't *Let's Make a Deal.*"

"That was a cool show—I watch it on the Game Show Network. I wish it were still on. I'd go as a banana."

"Now you're trying to distract me."

"Maybe."

I turned onto my street and nearly crashed into a tree, I was so distracted by what was in my driveway.

A Dumpster.

With my bathtub in it.

"Looks like Grandma Cel has been busy."

I parked at the curb, behind Maria's Mercedes.

As I opened my car door I caught sight of Mr. Cabrera and Boom-Boom speeding down the street in her golf cart. She braked to a stop in my driveway behind the Dumpster.

"Having some work done, Miz Quinn?"

"I guess so, Mr. Cabrera."

"Need help?"

Maybe of the psychiatric kind, but I didn't think that's what he had in mind. "Maybe. I'll let you know."

Boom-Boom stood with Riley, inspecting his arm. I walked over to them, and she said, "I really am sorry about this."

"He's no worse for the wear," I said, wondering if that was a cliché. I decided not. I'd had a rough enough day already.

"I'm not sure if I should be insulted by that or not," Riley said.

Mr. Cabrera clapped him on the back. "Or not."

"When are you guys coming to Growl? Remember, dinner's on me."

"I couldn't," Boom-Boom tittered.

I didn't think it was possible to titter, but it was. And she did.

"Come on, you have to. I promised. And I never break my promises."

Unlike his father. Which got me to thinking about Kevin. And Bobby.

I missed him. Bobby, that is. Not Kevin. And I'd just seen him last night. Bobby, not Kevin.

What did this tell me?

"When are you working again?" Mr. Cabrera asked.

"Wednesday night. Five until closing at ten."

"We'll be there. It's a date."

Boom-Boom giggled and clasped onto Mr. Cabrera.

I couldn't help myself. "Did Riley tell you, Mr. Cabrera?"

"Tell him what?" Riley asked.

"That Mrs. Krauss is working for me temporarily? While Tam is out on leave?"

The color drained from Boom-Boom's face.

"How could I have told him that?" Riley asked. "I'm just now— Ow! Why'd you step on my foot?"

"Did I?" I asked. "Sorry."

"Ursula's okay, then?" Mr. Cabrera's blue eyes held a hint of worry.

"Of course she's okay," Boom-Boom trilled. "Old battle-axes like that never die."

My eyebrow arched. Riley's mouth fell open. Mr. Cabrera disengaged Boom-Boom's arm from his.

"I, er, mean that in the nicest possible way."

"Of course," I said.

"Nee-nah! You're home. You've got to see the plans."

Oh Lord. Maria.

I crossed the lawn. "Plans?"

"For your bathroom. What's that in your shirt? Really,

Nina, I could give you the name of a good plastic surgeon. You don't need to stuff. How . . . adolescent."

I growled and pulled the envelopes out of my shirt.

"Do I want to know?" Maria asked.

"No."

"Okay, then. Come see the plans. They're gorgeous. Just gorgeous."

I stopped dead in my living room. The ceiling where the dining room used to be before Aunt Chi-Chi renovated now had a very large, very gray stain in it. One that dripped onto a large tarp covering my hardwood floor.

"Minor," Maria said.

"Really?"

"Not to worry."

Oh, I was worried.

"Come, come. Come look."

"I need a minute." To . . . regroup. Maria wasn't happy with the delay. She pouted.

The phone rang as I passed it, heading for the back door. The caller ID listed a toll-free number. Telemarketer. I didn't answer, but it did remind me that I hadn't checked my cell lately.

I tracked it down, took it and Bill's letters out to Mr. Cabrera's gazebo.

The ivy he'd started up the sides of the gazebo had taken off, nearly reaching eye level. I'd convinced him to plant it, even though he hadn't wanted to. When I pointed out how rude it was to spy on others, he'd reluctantly put it in. But I noticed he kept trimming it back.

My voice mail had three messages. The first one was from Bobby, who told me he would be out of town for a few days, working on a hundred-year-old house near Columbus. Lots of scraping and prep work, so he'd be staying in a hotel up there. It would give me time, he said, to think about what he'd said.

The second message was from Tam. She'd been sprung from the hospital and was at home at Ian's farm in Lebanon if anyone needed her.

The third message, another from Bobby, simply said, "I miss you already."

I sighed and dropped the phone into my pocket.

For a few minutes I sat there staring at Bill's letters, wondering why I'd taken them.

I told myself that it was none of my business, but then my sense returned. It *was* my business. Absolutely my business. Bill and Lindsey duping me had made it that way. And the lawsuit and possible murder charges had cemented it.

Not that I had to worry about the lawsuit anymore. Unless there were family members eager to pick up where Greta had left off.

There was Noreen—would she pursue the lawsuit?

Both letters had been opened—by Bill, I assumed. I pulled a single piece of paper out of each envelope and stared at them long and hard.

The first thing I noticed was the font. Every little *i* was raised slightly above the rest of the text.

The first letter read:

I know what you are doing. It will cost to not tell. I will contact you again soon.

The second curled my toes.

You will call Taken by Surprise Garden Design and arrange to have the backyard of Russ and Greta Grabinsky landscaped at your cost.

I stared at the letters for a long time.

Bill was being blackmailed.

By whom?

What kind of oddball blackmailed for landscaping?

And what did the blackmailer know about Bill that he'd so readily do it?

Something with the accounting books? I could easily see them sitting on the table in the Grabinsky house . . .

Right near the typewriter.

I studied the font on the letters and envelopes. That's why it had been so unusual. It had been made by a typewriter. An old-fashioned one.

One just like Greta and Russ's.

And since I knew Russ's penchant for blackmail, I had to wonder if Bill had been blackmailed by Russ himself.

Twenty-One

Tuesday morning I sat at my desk, trying to massage the crick out of my neck. So far, no luck.

True to her word, the night before Ana had come over with some desperately needed ice cream. I'd stayed up too late fielding her morbid questions about Greta Grabinsky, and gotten a lousy night's sleep on my sleeper sofa.

With all the construction in the bathroom, my room was currently unusable.

Tuesday was normally my day off, but the thought of the bathroom demo had driven me from my house and into my office.

The choice between Brickhouse and remodeling was a close one, but I had work to catch up on, namely a hummingbird garden I was designing as a mini for the Alonzos. Rich Alonzo was a novice birdwatcher, and his wife Lena wanted to surprise him.

No matter how hard I tried, or how much I threw myself into my work, I couldn't help but think of Bill Lockhart.

With my theory about Bill and Lindsey purposely plotting Russ's heart attack shot to pieces thanks to those letters, I didn't know what to think.

They hadn't planned for him to have a heart attack. Hadn't wanted him dead.

Maybe my Clue-playing skills weren't as good as I'd thought.

Yet, someone was blackmailing Bill. Which meant he was doing something he wanted to keep secret . . .

Had it been Russ blackmailing Bill?

He'd been blackmailing Dale Hathaway. Why not expand?

I played with different scenarios.

Russ, with a lawsuit looming, needed to have his backyard cleaned up, cleared out.

Maybe he'd heard Riley talk about TBS at work?

Being as cheap as he was, he certainly wouldn't want to pay my lofty fees himself, so he blackmails Bill into paying them for him.

Brilliant, actually.

And Bill, desperate to keep his secret, has Lindsey call me, setting the whole thing into motion.

Grabbing a red-colored pencil from the mason jar on my desk, I shaded blooms on a carnival weigela—a red, white, and pink flowering shrub hummingbirds loved—as one thought continued to nag at me.

Why then had Russ seemed so surprised to find my crew and me at his house if he'd planned the whole thing?

I chewed on the end of the pencil. Had his reaction been orchestrated too? Part of the grand scheme?

The pencil fell from my fingers.

It fit!

Russ finds us there, pitches a fit, and a lawsuit follows.

Not only is his yard done free of charge, but he also possibly gets money from me, in addition to Bill and Lindsey, to settle a lawsuit.

Except he went and died, ruining everything.

Almost everything. Greta still threatened to sue. Almost immediately, as if it had been on her mind all along.

Which left me to believe that Greta had been in on it all.

I finished coloring the weigela and reached for the purple pencil for the perennial salvia.

Russ and Greta had been in it together. And if Greta knew about Russ blackmailing Bill, she must have known about Russ blackmailing Dale.

Had someone else figured this out? And decided to end the scheming for good by killing Greta since Russ had already conveniently died?

Had Dale killed Greta? Had Bill?

Setting the pencil down, I remembered that Bill's blackmail letters hadn't been signed. Did he even know who had sent them?

If not, then there was no link between him and Greta's death except for the accounting books.

But Dale Hathaway was a different story. I'd heard him threaten Greta myself. And it made me wonder how he'd found out Russ was his blackmailer. Had he confronted Russ?

The phone rang. Brickhouse answered.

I went back to coloring.

I loved designing bird gardens of all kinds, but especially hummingbird habitats. There was just something so special about them.

The habitat itself was going to be an island in the middle of the Alonzos' backyard. I listed materials on a separate piece of paper as I created.

The intercom on my desk crackled. "Call on line one."

"Who is it?" There were certain people I was actively avoiding today. My mother, for one. I couldn't take one more construction disaster. My sister, for another. Her plans had included so much froufrou-ness, my bathroom had ended up looking like a high-priced French spa.

I was not a froufrou kind of girl.

Kevin was someone else I didn't particularly want to talk to. I needed some space to decide how I really felt about him. Plus, since I found those letters, I felt like an idiot for suggesting that the Lockharts might have purposely planned Russ's heart attack.

"It's Noreen Pugh."

I only knew one Noreen. "I'll take it." After a second, I picked up the phone, hit the number one on the console. "Nina Quinn."

"Nina, this is Noreen, Greta's sister?"

"I'm so sorry about her death."

I heard a sniffle, followed by a watery "Me too."

"Do the police have any ideas what happened?"

It was wrong to pry, but I couldn't help myself.

"No, not yet."

"I'm sorry," is all I could say.

She blew her nose, then said, "The police had me go through her things, but I couldn't see anything missing. I spent quite a lot of time there so I know the place well."

I didn't mention the accounting books.

"I'm calling because while I was there, going through the house, a neighbor stopped by."

"Oh?"

Had it been Dale?

"Kate Hathaway."

"Oh?" Had Kate known Dale was being blackmailed by Russ?

"She informed me about the lawsuit, how it was still in effect. That's why I'm calling. Did you know Russ and Greta have a daughter?"

Conversation from the day Russ died came back to me. *Hasn't seen his kid in ten years.*

I caught myself twirling the purple pencil. I was picking up bad habits from Deanna. Back in the jar it went. "I didn't know, no."

"Well, it was always Greta's dream to leave this house to Francie. That's why she took such good care of it. The yard . . . it always embarrassed her, but Russ . . . he was cheap."

Just reinforcement that Russ had been the one to blackmail Bill. And that Greta might have known about it.

"I'd like you to come finish the yard."

I leaned forward. "Really?"

"As soon as possible. I don't want Francie to lose the one thing her mother had wanted her to have. And Greta really wanted her yard done right. Pretty." She sniffled. "You'd have made it pretty, right? Lots of color? Trees?"

"Yes. It would have been beautiful. Will be beautiful. Of course I can finish the job."

Even if Greta had known about the blackmail, I'd been paid for the job. And Noreen's grief more than made me want to help any way I could. Beyond that, I thought of a mother's love for her estranged daughter, of the gift she wanted to leave her.

And I thought of my mother, who had given me the gift of my bedroom while I could still thank her.

I wasn't so mad about the bathroom anymore.

We talked about dates and settled on Thursday. I'd somehow make it work with everyone's schedules, including Ignacio's.

"Would you like to see the plans? For the yard?"

"I'd love to, but I'm at Greta's cleaning things up."

Perfect. "I can stop by. I don't mind the trip out there."

"Really?"

"Really."

I felt a little bad because I had ulterior motives, but there wasn't enough guilt to change my mind.

I needed to talk to Dale Hathaway.

Hanging up, I took a long look at my design. It had a ways to go, but I already adored it.

Woof!

I jumped up, ran to my door, flung it open.

Woof, woof!

"I swear she smells you," Kit said, holding a straining BeBe by a short leash.

"I do not have a B.O. problem."

"Never said you did."

"But—"

"Dogs have a great sense of smell. She just knows yours."

"Oh." I looked around. "Where's Mrs. Krauss?"

"Who?"

"Brickhouse Krauss?"

His eyes widened. "What's she doing here?" Kit had worked on Mrs. Krauss's mini. I remembered how he'd slunk away when Mrs. Krauss starting yelling, leaving me to deal with her alone, the yellowbelly. I swear his scary image was all a facade.

"Working."

He paled. "Here?"

"Tam hired her."

BeBe whimpered. Giving in, I moved closer and let her slobber my hand.

"Nina, I don't know—"

"She's actually been . . . okay. It'll be fine. And it's just for a few months, until Tam is back."

The phone rang and BeBe went crazy. Brickhouse came

hurrying in the side door, carrying a trash can. BeBe worked herself into a frenzy.

Brickhouse glared at BeBe, pointed a finger. *"Anschlag!"*

BeBe stopped barking, cocked her head.

"Sitzen Sie!"

BeBe sat.

My jaw dropped.

Brickhouse answered the phone. "This is Taken by Surprise, Garden Designs, Ursula speaking . . . Do you think that's wise? Well, I don't. You, young man, need to get your life in order. Prioritize. Make some hard decisions and stick to them."

Kit's mouth dropped open.

"See that you do," Brickhouse said, then hung up. "What?" she asked when she looked at us.

"Who was that?"

"Jean-Claude's not going to be able to make it in today. He apologizes."

"You need to fire him, Nina," Kit said.

Mrs. Krauss clucked again, jabbed Kit in his chest. "Have you never had troubles? Have you never needed help? Have you?"

Kit didn't back down. "Of course."

"Right now that boy has no help. He has troubles and he's trying to do it his way. Soon enough he will see that all he has to do is ask, and he will see who his true friends are."

"Did he tell you what kind of trouble he's in?" I asked. All I could see was Jean-Claude on the corner in the Blue Zone doing God knows what.

"He did."

I prodded. "Well?"

"I'm not at liberty to discuss it."

I blinked. She stared.

I wasn't going to win this battle, so I said, "I'm going out for a while. Kit, I need you to organize everyone, including Jean-Claude. We're going to be finishing the Grabinsky yard on Thursday." At his look, I added, "I'll explain later."

BeBe sidled up to Mrs. Krauss, sat obediently at her feet.

"We'll also discuss BeBe later."

I grabbed my backpack and headed for the door. As the chimes rang out, I heard Kit say, "How'd you do that? With BeBe?"

Mrs. Krauss said, "It's all in the tone. Did those tattoos hurt? I'm thinking about getting one on my—"

I covered my ears and ran for my truck. I didn't want to know.

Deep purple-blue circles lurked under Noreen's Sally Jesse glasses, and I swear she'd lost weight because she didn't look as potato as before.

The pansies had perked up at least.

I followed Noreen into the house. "I can't stop crying," she said. "Who could have done this to her?"

"Maybe," I broached, setting my backpack down on the recliner, "it was a natural death. A broken heart, maybe?"

One eyebrow arched and the other dipped. "You're kidding, right?"

"That bad?"

"Worse. Know why she took such good care of this house? Because it was the only thing she had. It had been a wedding gift from our parents to Greta and Russ. The deed was in her name. Russ controlled everything else."

"What about when he died? Didn't he have savings? Life insurance?"

She sighed with disgust. "He left everything to a male heir. A distant cousin." She must have seen the horror on my face. "Exactly."

"Not even to his daughter?"

"Francie couldn't stand him. Left at eighteen and never looked back. Broke Greta's heart. Russ disowned Francie, acted as though she hadn't existed."

"And Greta stayed with him? Why?"

"I wish I knew, Miss Quinn. I really do."

My image of Greta continued to change. From victim to villain, back to victim again.

It didn't escape my notice that Greta was the one whose legacy was threatened by the HOA's lawsuit. It twisted my thinking.

Had Russ been behind the blackmail at all? Or had Greta been the mastermind?

I needed to talk to Dale.

The design plans were fairly straightforward, and I could tell Noreen was pleased with them. We made plans to meet there at seven A.M. on Thursday morning to finish the job I'd started last week.

Something Noreen said triggered a question. "You said Russ left everything to a nephew?"

"Cousin."

"Even his partnership in Growl?"

"Oh, no," she said, leaning against the doorjamb. "The agreement between Russ and Bill stated that upon death, the surviving partner gains complete control of the business. Growl is all Bill's now."

Twenty-Two

Dale didn't look happy to see me. I didn't take it personally. An air-conditioned breeze swirled around my ankles from his open doorway.

"What can I help you with? We're not interested in a yard makeover."

Not exactly the welcome wagon, was he?

"You don't need one. Your yard is beautiful as is." Nothing like a little buttering up to get what I wanted.

"Look I'm sorry to be rude, but I only get an hour for lunch." The blue in his striped tie matched his eyes. "I have to get back in a few minutes."

I cut to the chase. "I know you're being blackmailed."

His head snapped back as if I'd hit him. Well, maybe as if Kit had hit him. I didn't know if I had that much force in me. Over his shoulder, he called out, "Be right back, Kate," and quickly closed the door behind him.

His handsome face transformed into something dark and ugly. He grabbed my arm. "How do you know that?"

I twisted out of his grasp. "Don't touch me."

Long fingers dove into his hair. "I'm sorry. It's just—this whole thing has been crazy."

"I overheard you in Greta's kitchen the other day. The window was open, your voices carried. I heard you threaten Greta."

His eyes widened as my meaning sank in. "I didn't . . . I didn't kill her."

"No?"

"No!"

"But you did go through her house. Looking for?"

"The pictures."

"Of?"

"I'd rather not say."

"How did Russ contact you?" I asked.

"By letter. Anonymously. But it had to be him. Who else wanted that lawsuit dropped?"

"You never confronted him, face-to-face?"

"I did. Once. He played dumb."

"Maybe he didn't know," I suggested.

"Had to have. Who else would have sent that letter?"

"Greta."

His eyes widened. "No way." He shook his head. "No."

"Why not?"

"She was too . . . Mother Hubbard. No, it wasn't her."

"Do you still have the letters? Could I see them?"

"Why?"

"Comparison value."

"Comparison? You mean someone else was getting blackmailed too?"

I nodded.

"Who?"

I borrowed his line. "I'd rather not say."

"You're married to that police detective, right?"

Six more days. "Yes."

Worry lines creased his forehead. "Does he know . . . about the blackmail?"

"Yes," I lied. If Dale had killed Greta, I didn't want to be next on his list.

He raked his hand through his hair again, sighed. "I don't want Kate dragged into all this. She's such a private person. Good Catholic girl, you know?"

No need to point out that there were actually very few "good Catholic girls" out there. Maybe Kate was the exception.

I didn't want to think about the sins *this* Catholic girl had been chalking up, so I said, "When did you break in to Greta's?"

"Yesterday morning. I didn't think she was home. I'd been watching the house, hadn't seen any lights or movement for almost a day. The back door was unlocked. I searched almost all the downstairs before heading up. I went through the bathroom, then headed to the master . . . that's when I saw her."

"Why didn't you call 911?"

"She was obviously dead already. What good would it have done except to implicate me?"

"Did you see anything out of place while you were there?"

He shook his head. "If your husband finds the pictures . . ." He closed his eyes. "They're going to become evidence, aren't they? Open to the public to examine and judge."

My curiosity buzzed. "Probably. Sorry."

"I'm glad Russ is dead. I hope he burns in hell."

On that cheerful note, I backed away. Fury glowed in Dale's icy eyes. "The police," I said, "will probably be by to talk to you soon."

He nodded. "I figured. I guess I need to take the rest of the day off."

It wasn't the stereotypical response of a murderer, which made me think that Dale hadn't killed Greta. Or maybe he was a good actor. Maybe I was gullible.

I needed to call Kevin as soon as possible and tell him what I knew.

"Can I see the letters?"

"I don't think so."

"Why not?"

Redness colored his cheeks. "They describe the pictures taken."

"Were they typed?"

"On an old-fashioned typewriter. Like the one Russ owns."

"Or Greta," I said.

"I don't buy it."

"Did you notice anything about the font?"

"The lowercase i is out of alignment."

Yep, they were written on the same typewriter.

"Anything else?" I asked. A confession, maybe?

"Wait a sec." Dale ran into the house, came out a second later. "Take these with you. I don't know why I took them in the first place except I knew Bill had been looking for them."

He placed two red leather-bound accounting books into my hands. So Bill hadn't taken them. He probably hadn't been in the Grabinsky house at all. Probably hadn't killed Greta.

But who had?

I called Kevin from my truck. I got his voice mail and thanked my lucky stars. I left a quick message about Dale Hathaway being blackmailed, possibly by Russ or even Greta herself, and casually mentioned that Dale had been the man I overheard threatening Greta.

I didn't mention Dale's breaking and entering into the Grabinskys' house. Kevin was smart. He'd put two and two together.

I hung up feeling as though I'd done my civic duty.

The accounting books sat on the seat next to me, in between a terra cotta pot and a roll of Mentos. I reached for the Mentos and tried to decide what to do about those books.

Technically, they belonged to Bill. But I couldn't shake the feeling that Russ had been suspicious of them in the first place. Had Bill been swindling Growl? Had Russ found out?

And instead of calling him on it, he turned to blackmail?

It didn't make sense to me. Why not just go to the police? That way Bill would be out of the picture for good, and Growl would be all his.

The accounting books slid on the seat. Suddenly I remembered something Lindsey had said.

That Greta had been a bookkeeper when she'd met Russ.

Was she still? For Growl?

That would explain the old-fashioned accounting books, rather than a computer program.

Who to ask? Who to ask?

I could call Bill, but after the heebie-jeebies I'd gotten from him the other day, I didn't think he'd be too open to any of my questions.

Lindsey? I doubted she knew much of what happened at Growl.

Noreen. She'd know, what with working at Growl and being Greta's sister and all. I called her house before I realized she was still at the Grabinskys'. I dialed 411 for the number there, but learned it had already been disconnected.

I called her house again, this time leaving a message asking her to call me back when she got in.

As I drove toward the office, I played with what ifs.

What if Greta was Growl's bookkeeper and had found an accounting error? Would she tell Russ about it? Or use it to her advantage?

Maybe blackmailing Bill was her way of getting out from under his control. A way to get what she wanted without having to deal with Russ at all.

In each case of blackmail, both Bill's and Dale's, Greta was the person getting something out of the deal.

And what if she knew having a backyard makeover would send Russ into cardiac arrest? Had that just been icing?

It was a lot of supposition and speculation and not enough facts. And it left wide open the biggest question of all.

What happened to Greta?

I turned a corner too fast, and the accounting books slid my way. I caught them before they went over the edge of the seat.

One of the books opened, and as I stopped at a red light, I scanned the numbers and columns, all of it jibberish to me.

My inner voice nagged that I should hand them over to the police. They might be evidence.

Might.

There was one way to know for sure.

Tam.

She'd done my accounting before business skyrocketed and I'd hired out. She'd probably be able to decipher the books, let me know if there was anything hinky in them.

I called her immediately.

She didn't bother with niceties. "It's on the news. The death of Greta Grabinsky. They mentioned TBS."

I groaned.

"Maybe you're jinxed. Just like your neighbor."

Oh my God. She was right. I was jinxed like Mr. Cabrera. People kept dying around me, left and right.

"Maybe you need to move. Get away from him."

And leave Aunt Chi-Chi's house? The Mill? I couldn't. I loved it there.

"It's all a coincidence, that's all."

Oh no. I'd gone and broken a commandment.

"Jinxed."

"Tam!"

"Oh, all right. It's a coincidence," she said, clearly not believing it.

Time to change the subject, before Tam had a real estate agent at my door and my house on the market. "How are you feeling?"

"I'm bored to death," she said. "I'm missing TBS. Someone is keeping your desk orderly and stocking the fridge, right?"

I had no idea. "Yeah."

"Are you lying to me?"

"I'd never."

She sighed. "It's lonely out here. The hospital was much more fun. People always dropping by. Thanks for sending your mom, by the way. She's a blast."

I did have a pretty good mom, on the whole. "I'm glad I could share."

"How's Ursula doing?"

"BeBe likes her."

"BeBe likes everyone."

"She's fine," I said. "She'll do until you get back."

"Aww. I just got warm and fuzzied."

"How bored are you?" I asked.

"I just finished alphabetizing the spice rack. Why do you ask? Do you have something you need me to do?"

The eagerness in her voice made me smile. "I might." I explained about the accounting books.

"I'm your girl. Bring them by."

"You sure you're up to it?"

"Nina, don't make me beg."

"All right. Let me check on Riley and I'll be up, and I can stay for a while." I hated thinking Tam was lonely.

"Is he working, by any chance?" she asked.

"No, why?"

"I'm craving something earthy. Growl does a great earthy."

"Yuck!"

"Don't knock it till you try it."

"How about I stop there and bring you something. What do you want?"

"Surprise me. But nothing that's going to kill me."

"I didn't kill those people! Besides, if I were jinxed, you'd be long gone by now."

"True enough. All right. Thanks. Hospital food isn't my favorite."

Really, it was the least I could do. I just hoped Tam could shed some light on Growl's finances, and if they could possibly be a motive for murder.

Twenty-Three

By Wednesday afternoon I hadn't heard from Tam. I'd left her the night before with the books, a large bowl of Asparagus Delight, and a Dandelion Fritter.

I spun in my swivel chair and looked out the window behind my desk onto the garden showcase beyond. Despite the beauty of the cottage garden and the water garden, my gaze always went to the xeric garden. I zeroed in on a yucca as I thought about Greta and Russ, Bill and Lindsey, and Growl. From the get-go, a partnership between two complete polar opposites seemed doomed. Then why go into it?

What had they each gotten out of it?

Russ got the restaurant he'd always wanted.

And Bill? What had he been in it for? Money?

I spun back to my desk, looked at the design for the hummingbird garden. I'd spent most of the morning surfing the Net for just the right accessories. I'd printed out pictures and was doing my best to replicate them onto the design board, using paints.

Little tubes of water colors covered my desk, and I used a paper plate as a palate. I mixed yellow, orange, and brown until I came up with an acceptable bronze color.

I glanced at the phone. I hadn't heard from Kevin.

Or Bobby, for that matter.

When would I stop lumping the two of them together?

By the time I looked up from painting, it was four-thirty. Riley had to be at work at five.

I cleaned up, made sure everything was ready for the morning, and said good-bye to Brickhouse, the only one left in the office.

I hated to say it, but she was an excellent temp. She'd even managed to get Jean-Claude in on time that morning. How, I had no idea.

Riley was pacing the front porch when I pulled in. He jumped in the car before I even came to a complete stop.

"Sorry I'm late," I said.

"You're not."

"Not what?"

"Late."

I must have looked confused because he said, "I told you I had to be at work at five, but it's actually five-thirty. That way I'd get to work on time. For a change."

"That's sneaky."

"It worked."

I didn't want to know how long he'd been playing that game with me.

I pulled into Growl's parking lot and was surprised to see the Beast, aka Mr. Cabrera's 1970 Pontiac LeMans, parked there until I remembered Mr. Cabrera and Boom-Boom had made plans to stop by.

Riley jumped out of the truck before it came to a stop, and I turned off the engine and double-checked to make sure I had Bill's letters. It was time to put them back.

Tempting aromas of garlic and thyme welcomed me in. And I was tempted. But not crazy, so I didn't buy anything.

Mr. Cabrera and Boom-Boom, however, were in line, ordering from none other than Goosh himself.

Boom-Boom was saying, "I'll have the turkey burger with lots of mushies. I just love mushies. Don't you?" she asked Mr. Cabrera.

"No," he said. "I hate mushrooms."

He wore a light green shirt covered in mallard ducks and denim cargo shorts. His tone told me that Boom-Boom was wearing on his patience.

I said hello while I scoped out the place. So far, no sign of Bill.

Mr. Cabrera turned to me. "You gonna eat, Miz Quinn?"

I wondered what Mrs. Krauss thought of him saying things like "gonna." How those two got along, I'd never know.

"No, not my style."

He smiled. "No chocolate."

He knew me well.

"I'm just dropping off Riley. Thought I'd, uh, use the ladies' room."

I could feel the sharp corner from an envelope scratching my spine. I'd shoved the letters in my waistband.

Mr. Cabrera gave me an odd look.

Okay, it might have been Too Much Information.

"Donnie, dear. Pay the boy," Boom-Boom trilled (I swear she did), while tugging on Mr. Cabrera's sleeve.

"Donnie?" I asked.

"Don't say nothin'," he grumped.

I smiled.

"And stop smilin'! Don't you have a bathroom to go to?"

"All right, all right. Testy."

I inched away, making sure the coast was clear, and saw Riley coming down the hall, his name tag on. He must've just punched in.

He caught sight of me lurking. "No," he said.

"What? I just need to use the restroom."

"There's peo—"

Mr. Cabrera's shouts cut him off. "What kind of scam are you runnin'?"

Riley and I both rushed back to the dining area. Mr. Cabrera saw us and said, "Trying to charge me fifty bucks for two sandwiches."

Boom-Boom's eyes were wide, her hand on her heaving chest. "Donnie, maybe you misunderstood."

We all looked at Goosh. Red-faced, he said, "Fifteen?"

"No, no," Riley said. "It's on me. My treat, remember?"

"What a sweet boy you are," Boom-Boom twittered.

Mr. Cabrera still looked ready to jump over the counter and do Goosh harm. "The boy's not right," he said under his breath to me.

He wasn't. Wide pupils, scattered thoughts, herky-jerky movements. Where was Bill? Couldn't he see that his head cashier was on something?

Goosh said to Riley, "Dude, you sure?"

"Yeah, of course."

While Riley dealt with the mess at the counter, I moseyed down the hall. After checking to make sure it was clear, I dashed into Bill's office.

A third barrel of mushrooms had appeared sometime during the last two days, which meant there was nowhere to hide if I needed to.

Working fast, I put the envelopes back where they belonged.

My palms sweated, my heart rate tripled. I fumbled a lot.

I closed the closet door, ran to the office door, poked my head out. I heard voices. Male ones. Coming my way.

I jumped into motion, slamming through the swinging door. I pushed open the ladies' room door just as the swinging door revealed Bill and two suited men entering his office.

Letting out a deep breath, I couldn't help but notice how close that had been.

After a second I opened the door, peered out. No one was coming.

I edged down the hall, nudged the swinging door a smidge so I could hear what was going on in Bill's office.

From what drifted out, the men were with the prosecutor's office, asking questions about Russ's death.

Great. Was I next on their list?

"Hearing something good, Miss Marple?" someone asked, his breath tickling my ear.

By the drop of my stomach, I knew that someone.

"You shouldn't sneak up on people!" I said under my breath.

Kevin pulled me down the hallway. "You shouldn't eavesdrop."

"I wasn't eavesdropping."

"Then what were you doing?"

"Um, looking for the ladies' room?"

He bypassed the dining room, put his hand on my back and steered me outside.

"Care to explain?" he asked. It was a cloudless day. The sun made his green eyes sparkle. Or maybe that was his anger.

"Not really."

"Nina . . ." he warned.

I explained. All about the blackmail letters, how they ruled out my theory that Bill and Lindsey had wanted Russ dead.

"I was going to tell you about them," I said.

"When?"

"After I put them back in Bill's office."

"Nina . . ."

"What? I found them by accident."

"Where?"

"Um, in his closet?"

"Are you asking me?"

"In his closet, okay?"

"Not okay. You've got to stop getting involved like this."

"I didn't mean to get involved!"

"You never do."

"What are you doing here, anyway?"

He looked like he knew why I was changing the subject, and appeared as though he was about to argue, but sighed and said, "Thought I'd stop in and see Riley. And remind him that he's at my place this weekend."

His place. Not his and Ginger's place.

Funny how saying that didn't bother me as much as it used to.

I guessed it was true, that time healed all things.

"What's wrong?"

"Nothing."

"Then why the pained face?"

"Cliché," I said.

He shook his head, grinned. "I'll never understand you."

"It's not your job anymore."

"And whose is it? Bobby's?"

Dangerous territory. "Maybe," I ventured.

"Look, I know I blew things with us."

I nodded.

"You don't have to agree so readily."

"Okay." I paused a few beats, then nodded.

"Better. Listen, Nina. I just want you to be happy."

This conversation was surreal.

Approaching footsteps caught our attention. Noreen.

"What're you doing here?" I asked.

Red-rimmed bloodshot eyes matched her glasses. "Bill called. Something about the prosecutor's office." She looked at Kevin. "Know anything about that?"

He shook his head.

He lied as well as I did. Scary.

Of course, I'd already known how well he lied.

I put my arm around Noreen. Grief surrounded her like Pigpen's cloud of dirt.

"Will you be okay?"

"Fine," she said, her upper lip trembling. "Sorry I didn't call you back, Nina. I've been—"

"It's okay."

"What did you have to ask me?"

I shot a look to Kevin. He folded his arms across his chest.

"Nothing that can't wait," I said.

"I'd really like to know too," Kevin said.

The two of them stared at me. "All right. I was wondering if Greta was the person who kept Growl's books."

Noreen nodded. "Russ was too cheap to hire out, even though Greta told him he should. Technology's just come so far since she worked."

Kevin stared at me.

I smiled.

"Why?" Noreen asked. "Did Bill ask you to ask me? I told him those books weren't in the house."

Kevin's eyebrows dipped dangerously low.

"Um, no. Bill didn't ask me. I was just curious, is all."

"Oh." Noreen looked confused.

"Yeah, oh," Kevin said.

Noreen touched Kevin's arm. "Any news on Greta's death, Detective?"

His eyes softened. "Nothing official."

Noreen perked up. "But something."

His tone softened. "Preliminary reports show she was poisoned."

"By what?" I asked.

"Looks like something she ate."

Noreen paled. "Poisoned?" Tears welled in her eyes.

"I'm sorry," Kevin said.

She nodded, pulled open Growl's door and disappeared inside.

"Autopsy results are being released to the media tomorrow."

"Any suspects?"

He arched an eyebrow. "Why don't you tell me? What's with the accounting question?"

"Nothing."

"Ever heard of obstruction?"

I shrugged. "I saw some accounting books in the Grabinsky house. Bill had been looking for them."

"When did you see them? When you found Greta?"

"No."

"No?"

"Before that. They weren't there the day I found Greta."

"You looked, then."

"I thought it odd that Bill wanted the books back so badly, that Russ even brought them home in the first place."

"What made you ask about Greta?"

How much did I want to tell him? All. All of it. I didn't want to carry the weight of this around with me. I explained about Dale Hathaway and the blackmail. About Bill and the blackmail. About the one person who had the most to lose.

"Greta," he said.

"Exactly."

I could see him turning over the situation in his mind. "Yet she's dead."

"Exactly."

"I need those blackmail letters."

"You'd have to ask Bill about that. Did you talk to Dale today? After I called you?"

"Yeah. Said he'd been blackmailed by Russ to drop the HOA lawsuit. He tried but wasn't successful. He thought bluffing with Greta about having it dropped would get his pictures back."

"Did he show you his letters?"

"Said he didn't have them anymore. Had thrown them away."

My eyebrow rose. I very much doubted that.

"Yeah," Kevin said, "I don't believe him either."

The door opened behind us. Bill escorted the two men from the prosecutor's office out of the restaurant. "Anything I can do, gentlemen," he said.

The two looked at Kevin, nodded in that way men do when they greet each other. Their attention turned to me for a brief moment, but they continued on to their black Ford Taurus.

I had the feeling I'd be seeing them again soon.

I still hadn't heard from Bobby's cousin Josh. I thought maybe I should put a call in.

Kevin pulled Bill aside, but the summer breeze carried their voices.

"I've become aware that you've been blackmailed. I need to see those letters, Bill."

Clearly shocked, Bill stammered. "How . . . ?"

"You don't need to know that. Why don't you show me where the letters are?"

Bill's shock turned into something else. For a second it looked like panic. "Now?"

"Why not?"

"I'm, uh . . . no."

"No?"

Bill pulled back his shoulders, lifted his chin. "You'll need a search warrant for that, Detective."

Kevin held his surprise well, I'd give him that. He'd be great at poker. "You sure you want to go that route, Bill?"

"I'm sure."

"All right, then."

Bill glared at me, then went back into Growl.

"He's not going to take this out on Riley, is he?" I asked.

"Not if he wants to live. What?" he said. "What's that look?"

"You're a good dad."

"But a rotten husband."

"Maybe you'll be a good ex."

"Five days."

Oh God. He'd been counting too.

"I'm sorry, Nina."

"I know."

I drove toward home wondering about Bill's evasiveness. Why not just show Kevin the blackmail letters? Was he afraid to admit why he was being blackmailed?

He'd have to eventually.

Unless he planned to get rid of the letters, deny they ever existed.

Too bad I'd made copies.

I wondered how soon Kevin would get a warrant. Probably not until morning. Our county judges were notorious for not liking to be disturbed at night unless it was an emergency of epic proportions.

Maybe Kevin could pull a few strings.

I'm sorry.

I was too. I was still torn about letting him go for good. My heart was still somewhat attached to him, like a painful sticky burr.

What I guess I really needed to decide was if I was ready to move on with Bobby.

Was I?

My cell rang, and I wondered if it was Bobby, if it was divine intervention telling me what I should do.

I looked at the readout.

Ana.

Bummer.

"Hey," she said. "Where are you?"

"Tylersville headed east."

"Turn around. Come pick me up."

"Why?"

"Jake called."

"Jake?"

"You know, the cute bartender. He knows what Jean-Claude's been up to."

"What?"

"Wouldn't tell. Said something about telling me over dinner."

"Was I even invited?"

"Well, no. But I need you there."

"Why?"

"To keep me in line. I'm really going to try to make this thing with Shakes work out."

"Okay."

"Thanks. Oh, and thanks for not making a joke about my commitment to Shakes."

I'd been so close. "No problem."

I banged a U-ey, was at Ana's in fifteen minutes. She bounded into the car in a turquoise camisole and a beaded miniskirt.

"What?" she said.

"You're not dressed like you're trying to work things out with Shakes." I took back roads to the highway.

"A girl's got to look good."

"Now you sound like Maria."

Ana made the sign of the cross. "Maybe I could put on a sweater."

"Do you have one?"

"No."

I rolled my eyes.

Ana and I speculated about Jean-Claude's job all the way to the river. I didn't bring up any dead people. Or lawsuits. Or blackmailers.

I needed a mental break.

People filled the seats at Paul Brown Stadium, and I wondered what event was going on there, since it wasn't football season.

My cell rang and Ana picked it up, flipped it open. "Nina Colette Ceceri Quinn's phone. . . . What?" Her concerned gaze shot to me.

"What?" I asked.

"We'll be there as soon as we can," she said, then hung up.

"What?" I asked, my palms sweating.

"There's been an accident."

I had a weird déjà vu feeling of Tam telling me the same thing.

"Not Riley?" I said.

"No. Mr. Cabrera and his new girlfriend. The girlfriend's dead. Mr. Cabrera's in the hospital."

I exited at the next off-ramp, got back on the highway and headed back to Freedom.

Twenty-Four

It was one of those hot muggy July days that just promised bad tempers and thunderstorms.

I looked around the Grabinskys' backyard and felt none of my usual excitement at starting a job.

Maybe because this job had been started, then put on hold.

Or maybe because today there would be no surprise at all.

Everyone must have felt the same way because they walked around like they were tiptoeing around a casket.

I shuddered at the creepiness of it all.

Ignacio and his crew were working with Kit on readying the yard for topsoil.

Kit had shown up this morning sans BeBe . . . and sans hair.

"I didn't like the staring," he said when I'd asked about it.

Like people didn't stare at the skull tattoo. I didn't press because, truthfully, I hadn't liked the hair.

It was almost ten and there had been no BeBe sightings. I was adopting a don't ask, don't tell policy where she was concerned.

Stanley Mack had enlisted Coby's, Marty's, and two of Ignacio's men to help with the deck. They were just starting with the support beams.

Deanna was due to arrive at noon, to oversee the flowers and shrubs.

The original sod had dried out, and Noreen hadn't wanted to pay for another load, so she opted instead to buy grass seed. The look definitely wouldn't be the same, but there was little I could do about it.

I'd seen her first thing that morning but not since. I hoped she was off eating something because she looked like she'd lost ten pounds in two days.

I found a quiet spot near the front porch and called the hospital. Mr. Cabrera was having tests done and wasn't in his room. Riley had stayed the night with him, refusing to leave his bedside. The two had a bond I didn't quite understand but respected.

Then I called Ana. Again. After dropping me at the hospital last night, she'd taken a taxi home to get her car and gone back to the Blue Zone alone.

I'd yet to hear from her.

Yawning, I clipped my phone to the pocket of my jeans and looked around at all that still had to be done.

It had been a late night. I'd managed an hour of sleep in a hospital chair, not nearly enough, and woken up with a crick in my neck.

My cell rang. My mother.

"*Chérie,* what's this I hear about Donatelli? The neighbors are all abuzz about it."

The neighbors being my neighbors. My mother was still overseeing the demo of my bathroom. Promises had been made about a Sunday finish.

"He's going to be okay," I said.

"I heard the woman didn't make it."

"No." The doctors had said massive head trauma caused her death.

"What happened?"

The accident had been witnessed by at least a half-dozen Mill residents, but it made it no less bizarre or easy to understand.

"Seems Boom-Boom and Mr. Cabrera had been on their way to the local cribbage game after dinner last night when Boom-Boom started driving her golf cart erratically and yelling about polar bears chasing after her."

"Polar bears? In the Mill?"

"I don't understand it either." Mr. Cabrera had been wearing a polar bear shirt the other day but wore mallards yesterday.

"Mr. Cabrera bailed out just as Boom-Boom jumped the curb and crashed into a tree."

"Do the doctors think she had a heart attack? Mrs. Daasch mentioned she had a heart problem."

"When were you talking with Mrs. Daasch?"

"She was walking her cute little fluffy dog this morning. Very sweet lady. Nasty dog."

I had to agree. Loofa looked angelic, but had a devilish personality.

"Tried to chew my Jimmy Choos."

"Mrs. Daasch?" I asked with a smile.

"Don't be a smart aleck, *chérie.* That lovely man across the street, the one with the flapping robe? He said Donatelli had broken an ankle?"

Flash Leonard. "Luckily that was all. They're keeping watch to make sure there's no internal injuries."

"Has Boom-Boom's family been notified?"

"I don't know."

"I'll see what I can find out."

Oh Lord. My mother fit perfectly in the Mill.

"And I'll organize a committee to make sure Mr. Cabrera is properly cared for when he gets home. He's going to have a hard time getting around."

"Thank you," I said.

"For what?"

"For being you."

"Don't get me teary. My mascara will run. I don't need raccoon eyes today. I have too much to do."

I smiled. "Sorry."

"Apology accepted."

"How's my bathroom?"

"What's that?" She made whirry noises into the phone. "You're breaking up."

"Good-bye, Mom."

"'Bye, *chérie*."

In truth I wasn't all that worried about my bathroom. I knew my mother would have everything under control. Eventually.

I called the hospital again. Mr. Cabrera was still having tests run. The doctors were trying to determine whether to operate on Mr. Cabrera's ankle or to just cast it.

What I hadn't told my mother, and what hadn't been spread around the Mill yet, was that the doctors suspected Boom-Boom had been under the influence when she crashed.

Of what, remained to be seen.

I started for my truck to grab the design plan when I spotted Meredith Adams marching my way. I turned and speed-walked away.

"Ms. Quinn! Ms. Quinn! I know you hear me."

I wanted to start sprinting. Two things stopped me. One was that my body was an aching mess between being knocked down by BeBe the other day and sleeping on that chair last night, and the other was I knew Meredith was tenacious. She'd probably chase me.

So I stopped.

"I assume you have all the proper permits to be working here?"

Kit had double- and triple-checked all the permits. We'd had to pull a few strings, and Kit even paid a little under the table to get it done, but everything was in order.

"Don't you have better things to do?" I asked.

Her cheeks turned red. Probably not from the heat. "Your disrespect for the rules of this neighborhood is abominable."

I looked over her shoulder as she lectured. A small white four-door pulled up behind the utility trailer. I knew that car.

I squinted as Mrs. Krauss got out of the car, tugged on something.

A black something. A big black drooling something.

Oh no.

I started for the car, but Meredith stepped in front of me.

"I have work to do," I said.

I caught Mrs. Krauss's eye. She looked upset. Again I tried to step around Meredith.

Again she blocked me.

I thought about pushing her down, but didn't want to be sued.

I heard Brickhouse say something in German, and BeBe took off, galloping toward us at full speed.

"Eee!" I screamed.

Meredith spun, saw BeBe, and dashed up the Grabinskys' front steps, plastering herself against the front door.

I braced myself for impact and was surprised when BeBe bypassed me and chased after Meredith.

Thoughts of more lawsuits flew through my head until another German phrase cut through the air and BeBe came to an abrupt halt and sat at the bottom of the stairs.

Brickhouse trudged up the lawn, handed me the leash.

"Are you okay?" I asked, despite myself. She looked horrible, with no makeup, white spiky hair every which way, and sad, sad eyes.

"I cannot do it."

"Do what?"

"Stay away. I tried. All night, I tried. But I cannot. He needs me and I need him."

Ah. Mr. Cabrera.

"I must go. Fire me if you must. I know you want to anyway."

"Um, excuse me," Meredith said. "Will he bite?"

I shrugged.

She moved toward the step, and BeBe lurched forward, but didn't go up the steps. However, she bumped into the pot of pansies, knocking it over. The terra cotta split in two, spilling soil all down the steps.

Meredith jumped back, banging against the front door.

I couldn't help but smile.

"This isn't funny," she said. "I'll sue!"

"Over what?" I asked. "Technically, you're trespassing."

She opened her mouth, closed it again.

My cell rang, but I pushed the silent button. "I understand, Mrs. Krauss. Just come back when you can. We will manage."

Her eyes widened in surprise. "Why are you being so nice?"

"Why'd you make me soup?"

She nodded and started walking away.

"Wait!"

She turned.

"What about BeBe?"

She said something in German, and BeBe trotted over to me, sat at my feet. Brickhouse bent down, looked in BeBe's eyes and said something I didn't understand to her.

"She'll be fine."

Out of the corner of my eye I saw Meredith dart down the steps, dash down the driveway.

"Tell Mr. Cabrera I said hi."

Mrs. Krauss patted BeBe's head and walked away.

I looked down at BeBe, held out my hand. She slobbered it. I smiled. Some things just didn't change. "You made a mess," I said to her.

She licked me some more.

I picked up the two pieces of terra cotta, set them aside. I scooped as much soil and plant as I could and carried it down the steps. I set the remnants in the grass and made a mental note to have Deanna find a place for it.

I turned to walk away when something sticking out of the soil caught my eye.

Bending down, I tried to make out what it was. Some sort of plastic. I carefully dug through the soil, trying to do as little damage to the roots of the plant as possible.

It took some doing, but I finally pulled it loose. A sealed plastic sandwich bag.

It held pictures.

A car door slammed, and BeBe went nuts. I slipped the pictures into my back pocket, turned and saw why.

Tam was standing on the sidewalk, one hand on her big belly, the other shading her eyes against the unforgiving summer sun.

"Tam!"

BeBe took off.

"Gesundheit!" I yelled, chasing after her, trying to catch her before she toppled poor Tam.

"Weiner schnitzel! Sauerkraut!"

Where was Brickhouse when I really needed her?

"Run, Tam! Run! Farfegnugen!"

When BeBe got within three feet of her, Tam held up a palm and said, "Stop."

BeBe stopped.

I huffed and puffed. "How'd you do that?"

"I have a way with animals."

She had on a pair of lime green capris and a large white T-shirt. Her hair was a mass of curls, her cheeks rosy.

She looked good.

"Aren't you supposed to be in bed?"

BeBe inched closer to Tam until she was practically a pair of drooling slippers. Tam patted her head.

"The doctor said I could resume normal activity. The baby's lungs are mature enough now so that if I do go into labor again, it will be safe to deliver."

"Are they sure?" I was a worrier by nature.

"They're the ones with the degrees. I just thought I'd stop by and see how the yard was doing."

"Are you going to come back to work?" I asked, hopeful.

Her curls bounced as she shook her head. "Think I'll rest until the baby's born. Don't want to push it. You're in good hands with Ursula."

Hmmph.

"Oh," she said. "I've got those books for you."

She opened her car door, leaned in and pulled out the accounting books. She talked as we walked to my truck, BeBe on our heels.

"At first glance everything seems to be in order."

"But?"

"It's really odd. On certain days of the week the store is barely floating by. On others, business is booming."

I thought about the possibility of Bill skimming from the days' takes. "Would those barely getting by days be Monday, Wednesday, Friday?"

"Actually, the opposite." She opened one of the books. "See here? This week last month, the profits on Monday, Wednesday, and Friday far exceeded Tuesday and Thursday. The weekends were somewhat of a wash. More was made, but not eye-poppingly so."

And the numbers were eye-popping. On the days Bill

managed Growl, he took in nearly quadruple what Russ had been pulling in.

"Does it look like someone's been embezzling?"

"Not that I could see," she said in that haughty way of hers that told me if she hadn't found something, no one would find something.

"Do you have any idea why the take would be so much higher on those three days?"

"Nope. Good management only goes so far."

"Weird."

"Very."

I stored the books in my truck, locked the door.

"How come BeBe is here? I thought Ursula was dog-sitting?"

At the sound of her name, BeBe's head snapped up, her tail thumped, and the drool flowed.

Eww.

I told Tam about Mr. Cabrera.

"Do you think Ursula and Donatelli will get back together now?"

"I don't know." But I hoped so. The two belonged together.

Her gaze lingered on BeBe. "Hey, why don't I take BeBe back to the farm with me? She can visit with her brothers."

Ian Phillips, Tam's new love, bred English mastiffs, and had raised BeBe from a pup.

She went to check with Kit, and I took the pictures out of my back pocket, unzipped the Baggie. There were three photos, taken at night. There must have been a full moon because the lighting was great.

I looked up at the Grabinsky house and decided that whoever took them—and I believed more and more that it had been Greta—had spied from the upstairs bathroom window. The one that overlooked the Hathaways' backyard.

In the pictures, Dale Hathaway was participating in a little nighttime nookie, poolside.

And I had to say, the man not only had amazing cheekbones . . . but cheeks as well. It was hard not to notice. The pictures seemed to be focused on his bare behind. Maybe Greta had a thing for cheeks too.

I flipped through the pictures, calling Dale every sort of bad name for cheating on Kate, until I spotted a shiny anklet on Dale's partner's ankle.

I knew that anklet.

Kate *was* the woman with him.

I silently took back the bad names as I remembered what Dale had said about Kate, about how shy and prim she was. A good Catholic girl.

If Greta had threatened to spread these pictures around the neighborhood, I could see why Dale would have gone to any lengths to protect her modesty.

My God. A man who loved his wife. Amazing.

I stuck the pictures into my back pocket and told myself I'd hold onto them until Dale was cleared as a murder suspect.

When—and if—that happened, he'd get them back.

As Tam loaded BeBe into her car, my cell rang. It was Kevin. Reluctantly I answered.

"Hypothetically," he said.

"What's with you and hypotheticals?"

"Bear with me."

Tam waved and drove away, BeBe hanging her head out the passenger window.

"I'm bearing."

"Hypothetically, if there were a search warrant to be served at Growl tonight, is there any possibility the missing accounting books might be found?"

"Hypothetically?"

"Of course."

I could drop them off there when I dropped Riley off for work. Hide them, maybe, so Bill wouldn't find them before the police did.

"Maybe."

"Maybe yes or maybe no?"

"Hypothetically," I asked, "if my prints are found on the books, am I going to be charged with anything?"

He groaned.

"Or Tam's prints?"

"You brought Tam into this?"

"I can wipe the books clean . . ."

"No! Don't do that. I'll deal with the fallout of the prints. Just be sure the books are there before eight tonight."

"A search, huh? Are you looking for anything else?"

"Good-bye, Nina."

I flipped my phone closed, noticed I had a message waiting.

"Hey. It's Bobby. I'll be home tomorrow afternoon. I was hoping we could meet up tomorrow night . . . to talk. 'Bye."

I clipped my phone to my pocket and caught my reflection in the window of my truck.

I was smiling like a fool.

A lovesick fool.

I pounded on Ana's door. Her SUV was in the lot and the lights were on. She had to be home.

"Let me in!" I shouted. "I have a key and I'm not afraid to use it!"

I heard the lock turn. The door opened slowly, and Ana stood there, wrapped in a robe, a bashful look on her face.

"I was going to call."

I barged in. "Before or after I worried to death?"

"Sorry," she said. "I, um, got tied up." She giggled. A male laugh came from the bedroom.

I rolled my eyes. I figured she'd gotten more than information out of Jake last night. So much for Shakes.

"I'm going," I said. I wondered if the search warrant had been served on Growl yet. I'd very cleverly hidden the accounting books in a printer paper box.

"So soon?"

"I just wanted to make sure you were alive. You are. Good-bye."

"Wait! Don't you want to hear about Jean-Claude?"

I hesitated. "Maybe."

"Sit. I'll make some popcorn. I haven't eaten all day. I'm starving."

I didn't really want to know what she'd been doing all day. I could guess.

And I was jealous.

"Well," she said, "I met with Jake at All Shook Up, and it turns out he'd arranged for Jean-Claude to show up after his set."

"Set?"

Ana stuck a bag of popcorn into the microwave, hit the Popcorn button. She leaned against the counter, waggled her eyebrows. "He works at Steel."

"Steel? Is that some sort of gym?"

Ana shook her head, smiled. "Nope."

"It's a strip club," a voice from behind me said. "I worked there during college to pay tuition. The pay is great."

To my shock, it wasn't Jake.

Nor was it S. Larue.

It was Dr. Feelgood.

I looked at Ana. "Shakes?"

She shrugged.

I groaned.

"Hi," Dr. Feelgood said to me. "I'm Johan Hornsby." He wore nothing but a pair of boxers. Looked to be the same ones I'd had on the other day.

The microwave beeped. Ana took the bag out, holding it carefully by the corner. "I came back to the hospital after meeting with Jake last night. You were gone by then. I ran into Johan."

I slid off my stool. "Hi," I said to him. " 'Bye. I'm going."

"Wait!" Ana said.

"What?"

"Jean-Claude. He wants to talk to you tomorrow morning, tell you everything."

I nodded. "You two have fun."

"Oh we will," Ana said, closing the door behind me.

Twenty-Five

I looked up from the hummingbird garden plans on my desk at the soft knock on my door. "Well, if it isn't JC Rock."

Jean-Claude sat in the chair on the other side of my desk. He rolled his eyes. "It's a stage name."

"But JC Rock?" I couldn't help but laugh. "It's such a stripper's name. You couldn't have been more clever?" I kicked myself now that I hadn't put it together before. Hindsight was evil.

"Stop. I heard enough from Ms. Bertoli." He fussed with a hangnail, said, "You're not mad?"

I shrugged. "I'm mad that you're doing a crappy job for me lately, but not because you're a stripper."

"Exotic dancer."

"Is there a difference?"

"My thong doesn't come off."

I held up a hand. "Too much information!"

He grinned. "Sorry. Look, I don't want to stop working for you, but I really need the money."

"I hear the money's good for str—exotic dancers."

"Better than I make here."

My jaw dropped. I knew how much Jean-Claude made working for me. It was a lot. "Really?"

He nodded.

Maybe I'd gone into the wrong business.

I tried to imagine my mother's reaction to her oldest daughter being a stripper. It wasn't pretty.

"Well, working both jobs isn't working out," I said.

"I know."

"Why do you need the money, Jean-Claude?"

Clearly uncomfortable, he shifted in his seat. "It's my brother."

Jean-Claude had two brothers who lived with him, one older, one younger. As far as I knew, there were no parents. "Michel?" Ana had dated him a few months ago. I didn't think it had gone much farther than a one-night stand.

"No. Henrí. My younger brother. He's fourteen." He looked me in the eye. "He's in jail."

I blinked. "In jail? At fourteen? Why?"

"Because he's stupid. Thought selling Ecstasy and mushies would get him the girl he liked. Now he's in juvie pending his trial. They want to try him as an adult, make an example out of him. He was just a stupid kid making a stupid mistake. I need the money to get the best lawyer possible. He deserves to be punished, but not like that."

Mushies. The word jumped out at me. I'd just heard that. Where? "What are mushies?" I asked.

"Street name for hallucinogenic mushrooms. Liberty caps, usually."

I nearly fell out of my chair. Mushrooms!

"Nina, you okay?"

It all came together so fast. Boom-Boom Vhrooman had ordered her turkey burger the other night at Growl with extra mushrooms. "Mushies," she had called them, probably oblivious to what she was ordering.

Oh my God. It all made sense now. Goosh. The closet of mushrooms. The blackmail. Bill was a dealer. Selling mushies through Growl.

I remembered how upset Mr. Cabrera had been at being charged fifty dollars for his and Boom-Boom's meal. It hadn't been a slip of the tongue by Goosh. He'd been charging Mr. Cabrera for the mushies.

Extra mushies, Boom-Boom had ordered.

"Can you O.D. on these mushrooms?"

"Well, yeah," Jean-Claude said. "They're like any other drug. You don't look good."

"Did you ever hear of a place called Growl?"

Eyes wide, he opened his mouth, then snapped it closed. After a while he said, "I don't really want to get involved in this."

"Too late."

"Listen, Nina—"

"Growl, Jean-Claude. What do you know?"

"Henrí mentioned it."

"As a place to get mushies?"

He nodded.

My God. No wonder Boom-Boom had seen polar bears. Had crashed.

It all made sense. The nighttime delivery. The extra income on the days Bill worked—he probably only sold the mushrooms on the days he managed. More foot traffic, more sales.

"How do you know about Growl?" Jean-Claude asked.

"My son works there."

"Oh."

I didn't even think of that! Was Riley involved somehow? I couldn't let my brain go there. Not yet. I needed to stay focused.

"Where does one grow mushies?"

"They grow everywhere naturally—fields, woods, yards. It's just a matter of being able to tell them apart from other mushrooms."

Woods. Like the ones behind the Lockharts' house? I'd seen mushrooms growing there the day BeBe got loose. "Would you know one if you saw one?"

"Well, yeah."

"Do I want to know how you'd know?"

"No."

"Okay, then." I stood up.

"Where are you going?"

"Where are *we* going," I said. "On a field trip."

It took fifteen minutes to drive to the Lockhart house. Another five to show Jean-Claude the mushrooms growing in the woods and for him to tell me they were harmless.

I'd been so sure.

"What now?" he said.

"Plan B." I walked out of the woods and couldn't help but admire the job well done in the Grabinskys' backyard. Even without the sod it was a hundred times better than what it was.

"What's Plan B?" Jean-Claude asked.

"Growl," I said.

"I don't think this is in my job description."

"Are you even still working for me?"

"Am I?"

"How about part-time? Afternoons? We'll work from there."

He smiled. "Sounds good. Um, how are we going to get into Growl? It doesn't open till later, right?"

I knew just the person.

Thirty minutes later a grumbling Riley was in my truck. "This is wrong," he said. "It's my day off. I wanted to sleep in."

"Nine-thirty is sleeping in."

"In old people's time."

"You calling me old?"

"If the Metamucil fits."

Jean-Claude laughed.

"You're not much younger than I am," I pointed out to him.

He stopped laughing.

"You can sleep in tomorrow," I told Riley.

"Ginger always wakes me up for pancakes."

"Life's tough," I said.

"Ginger?" Jean-Claude asked.

"Dude, don't ask her."

"Good advice." I pulled into the empty Growl parking lot.

Riley hopped out, let us in. "What are you looking for?"

"We'll just be a minute."

The office door was closed but unlocked. I turned on the light, pointed to the closet door. "Go ahead," I told Jean-Claude.

He opened the door. "What am I looking for?" he asked. "Mayonnaise?"

I peeked over his shoulder. Sure enough, the three barrels of mushrooms were gone.

I should have known! Bill knew Kevin would come back with a search warrant. No wonder he hadn't wanted to show Kevin the blackmail letters. Had he opened the closet, Kevin would have seen the mushrooms.

"Bill took them out two nights ago. Right after you and Dad left," Riley said from behind me.

I jumped. My heart pounded. "Don't sneak up on me like that!" Then I realized what he said. "Took what out?"

"The mushrooms."

"You knew about the mushrooms?"

"Not until you said you overheard him scheduling a delivery. I knew something weird was going on around here, but didn't know what."

"Well, it's of no use now. I can't even say for sure if they were the hallucinogenic kind."

"I've got one," Riley said.

"What!"

"I came in and took one that night. I had a feeling. I was just waiting to show Dad."

"Where is it?"

"At home."

I looked at Jean-Claude. "Plan C."

"Do I get a raise for this?" he asked.

"No."

I followed the two of them out the door and was just about to turn out the light when I spotted something on the floor, caught under the door.

The corner of an envelope. I tugged, ripping a gash in it. But the words on the front were still clear. "Bill Lockhart. Personal."

Maybe the officers executing the search warrant had dropped one of Bill's blackmail letters by mistake?

I turned it over.

Sealed tight.

The hair on the back of my neck stood up.

"Nina? You coming?" Riley called.

I stuffed the letter in my waistband, pulled my shirt over it.

As I closed up behind us I wondered how it was possible for Greta to blackmail Bill from the grave.

My mother was a bit surprised to see us back so soon. Very surprised, if the way she was blocking the doorway was any indication.

"Mom?"

"Yes, *chérie?*"

"Let us in?"

"Now's not a good time," she said, trying to look nonchalant.

Hmmm. What went wrong now?

"Look, there's Gérard Depardieu!"

Her eyes widened and she craned her neck. I pushed past her. Half my living room ceiling was on the floor.

"Whoa," Riley said.

I looked at my mother. "A little complication from the water leak the other day."

I practiced Tam's Lamaze breathing again.

Riley ran up the stairs, came back down a minute later, a hard-hatted man behind him. His tool belt jangled. "Mrs. Ceceri," he said to my mother, "the upstairs is not safe. Until we get a structural engineer in to assess the damage, the whole place really isn't safe."

My eyes bulged. I think a vein popped.

"Now now. Riley is staying with his father for the weekend. You can stay with us. I'm sure the problem will be cleared up by Monday."

Mr. Hard Hat looked like he wanted to debate that point, but my mother gave him the Ceceri Evil Eye and he backed away.

Stay with my parents. Oh, Lord.

My mother must have read my thoughts. "Or with your sister," she said.

A newlywed.

She sighed. "Or with Ana."

Not with a half-naked Dr. Feelgood hanging around.

"Our house, then," she said. "It will be fun!"

"You can stay with me," Jean-Claude offered.

I almost took him up on it.

"What's that you got there, Riley, *chérie*?" my mother asked. She pried open Riley's hand, stared at the mushroom.

"Yep, that's it," Jean-Claude said.

My mother's eyes widened. "Riley Michael. A mushie?"

I gaped at my mother. Was I so behind the times that she'd known what one was and I didn't?

"It's not mine," Riley said.

"Then whose is it?"

He thrust it toward me. "It's Nina's."

Hmmph. So much for "Mom."

Twenty-Six

I drove around until I finally found myself parked in the St. Valentine's lot. I figured fate had led me here, and I should go in and see Father Keesler and get it over with. Instead I cranked up the air conditioner and tried to think clearly.

I'd dropped Riley off at Kevin and Ginger's early. And I left Jean-Claude at TBS. He'd volunteered to man Tam's desk for the day, and I took him up on it. There had been a message from Kit, calling in sick. He had the flu.

I'd called him back. He sounded terrible. "And BeBe won't stop licking me."

"She just loves you."

"You've been waiting for that, haven't you?" he said, coughing.

"All week."

Icy air blew my hair around my face. I gathered it back into a ponytail and held it there.

Facts. I needed to weigh the facts.

Bill was a drug dealer.

Bill was being blackmailed.

Dale was being blackmailed.

Russ was dead.

Greta was dead.

Poor Boom-Boom Vhrooman was dead. I couldn't say I was going to miss her, but I still felt bad that she'd died.

Bill's illicit activities, his blackmail, and Boom-Boom's death were definitely tied together.

Dale's blackmail only related because his letter and Bill's were identical in appearance.

The same person, right?

I'd thought so. Until I found that letter in Bill's office this morning.

I wiped sweaty palms on my jeans, reached for the blackmail letter. Slowly, I opened it.

> BILL, DEPOSIT THIRTY-FIVE THOUSAND DOLLARS IN THE FOLLOWING ACCOUNT BY NOON FRIDAY OR I WILL GO TO THE POLICE.

The account was to a local bank, the numbers meaning nothing to me. I thought about calling the bank to get more information, but knew I'd never get anywhere without a name to go with the account.

Though I had a pretty good idea who it belonged to.

My cell rang. Kevin. "Just talked to Riley," he said.

"Oh?"

"What have I told you about breaking into places?"

"Not to leave my prints behind. Besides, it wasn't breaking. We had a key."

"Nina, if I have to put you in lockup, I will. A murder investigation is going on. Stay out of it."

"Murder? Did Russ's tox reports come back?"

"His and Greta's."

"That was fast."

"I don't question. I just appreciate."

"Was Russ murdered? Did he have hallucinogenic mushrooms in his system?"

"No. His reports were clean. He died of a heart attack. Plain and simple."

Surprisingly, my inner voice didn't have anything to say.

"Not so simple if I'm going to be charged with his murder."

"You're not."

"I'm not? When did this happen?"

"The prosecutor's office decided that since you weren't perpetrating a crime when Russ had his heart attack, they wouldn't charge you."

I slumped back in pure relief. "And Greta?" I asked. "What about her tox reports?"

"Ever hear of a death cap?"

"The mushroom?"

"Highly toxic."

"Someone poisoned her with a death cap?"

"It was in the soup she'd eaten for dinner. Evidence collected at the scene supported the findings."

I remembered seeing the Growl soup bowl in the trash, little bits of mushrooms clinging to its sides.

"We're interviewing people at Growl, seeing if anyone remembers Greta coming in. So far no one does."

In a flash I saw that Growl bag, the fisted hand that held it. "You won't find anyone."

"Why not?"

"Russ brought that soup home the day he died. He'd been feeling sick, came home early from work, had a Growl bag in his hand. He brought the soup inside the house, came back out to yell at me and very inconveniently drop dead."

"Are you sure?"

"Quite sure he died."

Kevin sighed. "About the soup?"

Sometimes it was so fun to play with him. "Not one hundred percent. But it's too much of a coincidence and I don't believe in coincidences."

"Yes, I know. It's a commandment."

"Don't mock my commandments."

"I wouldn't dream of it."

"You know what this means, right?" I asked.

"What?"

"That soup was meant for Russ. Not Greta. Someone had been trying to kill him, but the heart attack beat them to it."

After a pit stop at the parish rectory, I headed toward the Grabinskys' house. All the way there I hoped I was wrong about Noreen. I liked to think I had a good sense about people, and she'd struck me as the decent sort.

The sort that needed a makeover, but a decent sort nonetheless.

Even though Kevin had warned me to mind my own business and let him handle Noreen, I couldn't let it go.

I'm not sure why, so I just accepted it as a character flaw.

It was all there, plain as day now that I knew what I'd been looking for. Noreen had access to the Grabinskys' typewriter; she knew what was going on at Growl; she hated Russ. She'd been working the morning he'd gone home sick. Perfect time to poison his soup. Above all else, she had loved her sister and wanted her to be happy.

By having her backyard redone. By getting rid of a jerky husband.

How much had Greta known? Had she been in on it all along?

I checked my dashboard clock. Almost noon now. Was Noreen waiting for that money transfer? To leave town?

Emergency vehicles lined the street in front of the Grabinsky house. Paramedics roamed the yard. Patrol officers were roping off the sidewalk to keep gawkers at bay.

Meredith Adams stood along the fringe. "What's going on?" I asked her, not having a good feeling about this at all.

She stuck her nose in the air, sniffed, and said, "This neighborhood was perfectly respectable until you came along."

Yeah, it was all my fault. "So, I shouldn't buy the Lockharts' house?"

Her eyes went wide, her mouth dropped open. "You wouldn't."

"I might," I lied.

She turned on her heel, stomped away.

A body covered with a white cloth was being carried out of the house on a stretcher.

It was a lumpy body. Potato-shaped. "Oh no."

Weaving and bobbing my way through the crowd, I finally found Kevin. He pulled me aside, to a quiet corner of the driveway. I handed him the blackmail letter and he slipped it into a plastic evidence bag.

"Suicide," he said. "Left a detailed note. Couldn't live knowing she was responsible for Greta's death. She knew Greta had successfully blackmailed Hathaway and thought she'd try her hand at it with Bill. She knew about the mushrooms. Left us names and dates to help put him away. She admitted to putting the death cap in Russ's soup. She hoped his death would look like a heart attack brought on by the makeover. That no one would be suspicious. That there'd be no autopsy. She hadn't counted on Greta being so grief-stricken."

"So Greta didn't know about the makeover?"

"Apparently not."

"Who was the money for?" I asked.

"Greta's daughter. To pay off HOA's fees."

"What's going to happen to Bill?"

"The prosecutor's building a case against him."

I looked over to the Lockhart house, saw Lindsey on the front porch. I thought back to why I'd taken on the makeover in the first place, just to learn more about Kevin's first wife.

I'll admit I was still curious, but it was time to let the past go. For good.

"You have a place to stay tonight?" Kevin asked.

"My mother offered."

"That desperate?"

"Getting there."

"I better get back." He walked away, then stopped. "We never did find those pictures Greta used to blackmail Dale Hathaway. You don't happen to know anything about that, do you?"

"Not a thing."

One of his eyebrows rose. He nodded once and disappeared into the Grabinskys' house.

I made a stop at the truck, then worked my way through the crowd over to Dale Hathaway, who was sitting on his front porch.

"I can't believe it," he said.

"It's terrible." And rather ironic since Russ went and died on his own, making all the blackmailing and murder plans for naught.

"Where's Kate?" I asked.

"At the doctor's."

"Oh no—she doesn't have that flu, does she?"

He beamed. "No. Just a checkup. We're having a baby."

"Congratulations."

"Thanks." He looked down at his hands, then back up. "I'm being arraigned on Monday."

"The breaking and entering?"

He nodded. "With a plea deal, I'll get probation."

Ana would probably have him in my office by the end of next week looking for a job.

I slipped the pictures out of my pocket, handed them to him. "An early baby gift."

His light blue eyes widened. "Where'd you find them?"

"Doesn't matter."

"Why not give them to the police?"

"Noreen's suicide note all but seals the case. There's no need to have these pictures passed around the squad room."

"I can't thank you enough," he said.

"No need." I stood. "Just keep loving your wife."

"That I can promise."

I looked up, saw Kevin standing in the Grabinskys' driveway watching me.

After a second he turned and walked away.

I rolled over in bed, answered the persistent ringing of my cell phone.

Under other circumstances I'd have let it ring, but with Tam being so close to delivery and Mr. Cabrera still under observation, I couldn't ignore it.

A warm hand reached out, rubbed my bare back as I answered. "This is Nina Quinn."

"This is Josh Drake," the voice on the other end of the line said.

Josh Drake? Who was Josh Drake?

Lips pressed against my spine.

Okay, I didn't care who Josh Drake was. I just needed him to get off the phone so those lips could press other places.

"Sorry, I think you have the wrong number."

"I don't think so," the man said.

I wasn't in the mood to argue the point. "Can I call you back?"

"Actually, I'm looking for Bobby. Is he there? Because he's not answering his phone. It's important."

Josh . . . Oh, Josh Drake! Bobby's cousin—the lawyer.

I looked over my shoulder, at the naked man in bed with me. "For you."

"Now?" He grumbled about lousy timing.

"Apparently. It's Josh."

Bobby leaned up on his elbow, took the phone. It was my turn to distract him. Fair's fair. Besides, it was fun.

"Uh-huh," Bobby said, unable to take his eyes off me.

I could hear Josh talking a mile a minute, but I couldn't make out exactly what he was saying.

"Yeah, I promise," Bobby rushed to say. "Whatever you need, Josh, I'll do. I'll call you tomorrow for the details."

The phone landed on the floor amidst the pile of hastily discarded clothing.

Bobby pulled me close to him. "Where were we?"

"What did you just promise him?"

"Don't know, don't care," he said, leaning down to kiss me.

"Right then and there, I didn't care either.

If we'd only known.

Take Your Garden by Surprise

by Nina Quinn

Creating habitats for hummingbirds, or hummers, isn't only a rewarding gardening experience, but it can provide hours of enjoyment watching these amazing colorful creatures that average less than four inches long in size.

To build just the right environment, you need to keep in mind what hummers need most. Food, water, shelter. Providing extras such as shade in the summer, protection in the winter, places to hide, perches to rest, and space to flutter free of worries, will increase your chances of drawing hummingbirds to your yard.

Although hummingbirds are naturally attracted to the color red, they will be drawn to any nectar-rich plant, as nectar is their primary food source. Therefore it's important to choose the right varieties of flowers, shrubs, and trees for your hummingbird garden. Below are some good choices.

Annuals: impatiens, begonias, petunias, red salvia, geraniums, scarlet sage, penstemons, four o'clocks, velvet trumpet flowers, phlox, nasturtiums, zinnias.

Perennials: columbine, hollyhock, bee balm, trumpet honeysuckle, hosta, coral bells, cardinal flower, foxglove, dragonflower, monarda, aster, perennial salvia, verbena, cosmos, dahlias, delphiniums, flame acanthus, fuchsia, lupines, monkeyflower, sage, scarlet sage, butterfly weed.

Vines: trumpet creeper, trumpet vine, scarlet morning glory, bougainvillea, cardinal climber, flame vine, lantana.

Shrubs: Fuchsia, azalea, butterfly bush, abelia, bottlebrush, hibiscus, lilac, weigela.

Trees: mimosa silk tree, crab apple, willows, tulip poplar, locust, eucalyptus.

Research is a must. Not only to check to see which plants will grow in your hardiness zone, but also some varieties (such as phlox, penstemon, four o'clocks) could be annuals in some areas, perennials in others; and some perennials could be shrubs in some zones. Visit your local garden centers—they can point you in the right direction and might have additional suggestions that will make your hummingbird garden perfect.

Additionally, it's important to supplement your hummingbird gardens with feeders for the times nectar might run dry. The standard mixture is four parts water, one part refined sugar. Be sure to boil the water before mixing to ensure proper measurement and to purify the water so the hummingbirds don't contract any illnesses. You can also buy ready-made hummingbird food at any bird store and often in your local supermarket pet section. Never add honey to your hummingbird feeder. It can grow a fungus disease that can be fatal to these birds.

Hummers also eat insects and spiders, so be sure never to use pesticides in your hummingbird garden. Pesticides will not only remove an important food source but can also endanger a hummingbird's life.

It's important to keep a mister, dripper, or shallow bird bath near your hummingbird garden so the hummers can bathe and keep hydrated. Did you know hummingbirds drink eight times their body weight a day?

Hummingbirds won't use houses—they nest in trees—so don't bother buying one. These birds spend eighty percent of their time resting, so make sure they have perches near their food source. Twigs, branches, fences, clotheslines, or even nearby trees will provide the rest your hummers will need.

Remember to space your plants to accommodate fluttering wings, which can beat twenty to two hundred times per second. Research, plant, and sit back and enjoy your hummingbird garden year after year.

Best wishes for happy gardening!

Investigate the Hottest New Mysteries!